The Hanging Of Humanity
By
Mike Keane
Copyright © Mike Keane 2021
All Rights Reserved
Cover design by Mike Keane

The far away massacre in foreign lands wrapped in the rags of the slaughtered youth buried in the golden sand of fire,warm in the blood of crimes against humanity,another nail in the dusty coffin stained in the blood of tyrants dressed to kill with a wry smile on the face of shame;the butchered will rise again on the last day to flap in angelic wings through the glowing sky to spit fire on the wicked still alive in the cold grave;the son of man will kiss the righteous and the meek never to fade away in the grasp of humanity;the cold furnace without fuel to feed the fire in leaving the school of life,only for the stank teacher to abuse the children of innocence in the verbal slap of the fat hand to scar the greyness forever more in the lovely isle of green changing colour at the drop of a hat;the purest child trapped in the person possessed to wear the battered boots of the worn shoe,drift into an eerie silence of the big,bad wolf where the hungry fangs dig deep into the tortured soul;the slither of the slippery snake leaks venom on the flesh to have it all in the fat of the hand starved of dignity,the end of purity choked on the bitter pill in the dry swallow of life sizzled in the warped mind of the shady asteroid to crash into the thunderous head of the storm,smashing a divine retribution to repent in the ancient pew steeped in the forgiveness of prayer;sleep on the cold slab in a tearful reminisce of yore,watching the brightest day drift into the darkest night,startled by the violence of a storm on the run;blink when it's all too late to strike the humble match to light the fire of the eternal flame streaking across the weeping sky;

stare at the piercing light where the sun don't shine to cleanse yourself in the stagnant water of the frozen lake full in the polluted darkness of mankind;drink from the sweetness flowing o'er the glass jug to empty the bile of the ulcerated stomach into the dim light to shine in a glow of greatness dashing through the sky in the music of the night sphere;the end is nigh to spark the flame of the funeral pyre,a soft voice laughing in a fake smile in the turbulent rub of the cold hands;be conscious when you die,eyes wide open to stare death in the face before it takes you away with eyes wide shut in the gasp of the last breath,drifting into a new beginning,a new life in the bosom of the fluffy white cloud bouncing in the bluest sky,Etna blowing ashes of the soul on the stardust to protect the righteous meek in the bravery of a troubled life before entering the gate of wisdom still warm in the womb of existence;the celestial light now burning in the glow of the sleeping sun to caress the tired face of the morning sun with little eyes full of sleep,moist in the dew drop of nature taking its course on the beaten path of time;rest awhile on the wooden bench bent in old age to cuddle the creaking bones in the puff of the sweet smoke from the clay pipe,stare with bloodshot eyes o'er the mountain that gave you life,rub the itchy nose with the tobacco stained fingers in a raucous rumble to clear the skinny throat of a curdling phlegm,a spray of saliva to blow away in the wind of change,holding back the years of the old man snug in the wooden bench,a mist of sweet smoke wheezing through the shrinking lungs of the dry lips shriveled in the passing of time;once young in the echo of a vibrant buzz whizzing through the veins only to hit the buffers of old age staring you boldly in the face of the cracked mirror;stand stark naked in front of the brittle bones resting on the wooden bench to rub the tired eyes clear of the blinding mirage in the autumn of the crispy leaves leaving the branch on the tree of life;the confused mind wandering into a surreal wonderment trapped in the shadow,blink and all will be revealed in front of the naked eyes clutching at the straws of life screaming to leave in the milk of the leaking nipples of the beloved mother holding the crying child close to her warm bosom in the comfort of a soothing lullaby;the old man returns to rest in the beaten armchair to cool his anger of a life coming back to haunt him to the grave,a violation of the naked flesh in the disturbed mind,waiting patiently for the gentle stroke of the hand to arrive and walk away a happy slave on the mean streets paved in gold that turns to stone on the touch of the greedy hand,count the fool's gold in the rented bedroom of another on the run from the law;the demon addictions come back to tease you into a haunting submission to crawl around on bended knee crying for mercy to feed the hungry mouth covered in the glory of money under false pretenses watching the vulnerable wither away into a painful obscurity,cry not for the poor soul riddled in the self pity of a warped survival;never let it be said that you couldn't dust yourself down in the swipe of a wet rag soaked in the sweat of a brutal demise,only to drink from the empty cup full of a poisoned intent,the sore eyes turn into a rotten redness stuck to the tobacco stained fingers tapping on the stem of the clay pipe,yellow in the passing of time;a nobody suddenly becomes somebody in a smile on the laughing face,a narcissistic clap on the back to boldly shimmer into the fading light hiding in the shadow,the good die young,a fleeting smile turning into a crying laugh;the fisherman sinks the blunt hook deep into the jaw of the pouting fish snatched from the stream in a swooping leap on to the sandy bank where worms wriggle into the dry earth,the gaping mouth of the flapping fins suck in vain for air through the raw gills starved of life,leave the quarry hole forever more in the slap of the hand on the dripping head,lights out to jump into the sizzling flames of a blackened fire,spitting sparks on the sandy bank,the harlequin flesh of the rainbow crispy to the touch on the tobacco stained fingers,sound as a trout to feed the old man for another day in the life of a lone survivor;catch a fallen star tumbling into the sea of life to feed the fish in the stardust streaming across the universe with a message of hope and love for the faithful departed and the souls yet to be born in the same hand that taketh and giveth life in the breath of integrity for one and all;jump through the hoops of anxiety in a powerful surge through the pounding water flowing o'er the slippery tail to foam at the mouth of the pouting fish fighting for life to spawn in a bed of glory,only to start all over again in the chain of a vital survival;kiss the lips that kissed the world back to life;

never break the chain of smooth pebbles,stand shoulder to shoulder,hand in hand in the bed of glory, a gush of pure jelly from the loins of youth;gush,gush, gush to carrying on gushing deep into old age if one is ever allowed the privilege to sleep in the box room like a pet dog behaving to the command of the witch mad in the head,better to have a roof o'er the bald head than freeze on the cold street paved in a fool's gold,stare at the muddy water in the rusty bucket,worn and torn, watch your life swirling round and round in a vague ambivalence to eventually kick the bucket empty of all dignity in a fond farewell;a wet kiss on the parched lips longing for more love in the unrequited love of another's blindness,stuck to the white sheet in a speck of dirt,crash into the stone wall of life,full to the brim in the leaking barrel of ice cold water,still cloudy in the dirt of a hard life scraped away on the side of the mountain looking o'er the painful birth dragged into a life in the country to sow the seed of fruit in the kitchen garden,the dirt sprinkled in a coat of lead,a bed of roses slowly wilting in the choking gaze of thorny weeds full in the envy of evil intent on the honest land turned into a wasted garden for the naked to streak in the dead of the dark night;dream in the garden throughout the weary night in an aching silence,damp in a sticky sweat,awoken only when the cock crows loud in the dripping dew of the morning sky to greet the dawn of another day;drag the creaking bones to the breakfast table,rest awhile to slurp on the milky tea of a mother's love for the hungry child sat at the wooden table steeped in the aura of the ancestors floating in a misty shroud o'er the hidden garden where the mystic wind blows in a wall of silence to calm the tortured mind,amen;the old dog for the hard road,worn away under the pounding echo of the mighty hoof bellowing a choking dust into the dry throat of the wheezing lung;the hobnailed boot stamps a branded print on the shivering dust rolling on the worn road,paving the way for a brighter future for the puppy using the path,soon to bravely walk the hard road to find its way in the shadow of life,once so bright in the shadow of darkness,the little puppy still wags the tail to tickle the toes of the laughing child,who went to the market in the echo of the barking dog,now so old and grey to walk the hard road to the very end of the line,a long road without a turn or a twist in the tail;the evening sun going down behind the mountain in a glowing,goodnight smile to kiss the hard road on the dusty lips;the wall will never fall in a delirious tumble,driftwood lost to the deep sea crashing on the rocks to scar the slippery face of the battered cliff,the wall will never fall,hanging on to life like the old man leaning on the timber gate,the clay pipe leaking in a sweet smoke through the shriveled lips of time stuck to the grey face of the old man,gasping for a drop of porter to wet the aching thirst away,far away into the trampled distance branded on the hard road;the end is just around the corner,but never arrives on time,a derailed train left to rust on the empty platform, the steam still gushing from every crevasse,freedom at last to crawl from the wreckage,the aching body broken,succumb to the pain pounding through the body,refusing to leave like a possessed demon with evil intent,the weeping eyes plastered in a blind graffiti gone stone mad in the head,a bitter sweet pill to swallow in the crash of the mind into an empty schizophrenia,the flickering lights going dark in the manic screams of madness,help is nowhere to be found in the corrupt state of greed;the white stone rotten in the cavity of the soft tooth,spitting fragments into the storm of the roaring sea,slowly whipping life out of the cliff fading away into the deep,the trapped message in the bottle now covered in the fragments of the broken tooth,hell had no fury like the raging sea full in the anger of a desperate life;no more,please,no more pain in the valley of tears to lament in the sin of sins;the black beret turns red in the blood of the gaping scull,gushing out life in a lame demise;the white gaze alight in the black shadow streaming in the birth of an amoral equality within,without the rough chains digging deep into the open wound of old scars in a brutal life,the rape of the body and soul in the end of life as you know it;a faint whistle blows in the deaf ears of the dying,buried deep in a bed of roses,the perfumed scent lingering in the bleeding nose,waiting for the return of the forefathers to bury the dead;the bewildered watch themselves wither away in the dying embers frozen in the cracked ice of the stoked fire,a strange wander into the demented head that will never heal,the madness full in the grandeur riddled in the guilt of regret gurgling in the gasp of the last breath;a piercing pain in the arse of the ragged trousers,slipping down to the knee of the ankles pushing the shy feet to wildly dance on the cobbled streets lost to the choking city,drowning in a sooty fog,flick the trodden hat into the sodden air to land in the gutter to sleep with the rats on the run from the plague;bang on the ancient door to drum it open,leading you to the land of hope and glory in the free dance of the brave,the crispy leaves pave a path of gold for the chosen few,the leaves turn soft in the dry veins of the freezing night asleep in the flicker of the stars drunk in the glowing sky,the early morning dew drops cuddle on the naked,white scalp straddled in the combover of grey hair streaking on the head of the bald man ashamed of his fate;drop on bended knee to genuflect in the image of the cross to hide in the shadow where the sore eyes blink in a weeping remorse for the sins of yore;walls appear out of nowhere in front of you to block your way in life on the path trodden by other people,watching your every move in the colour of your money for people to take it away,out of your hands worked to the bare bone,moving stone by stone to stop you in your tracks on a dizzy journey through life,running into walls along the way;a stray dog on the hard road,emaciated in the rags of a broken man,weak on the feet dragging him around in circles,making him more dizzy to stumble into the wall of walls,the droplets of the dripping blood stain the scars slashed on the beaten face of a horrid experience on the road of hard knocks rising to greet you with the outstretched hand of a crooked smile on the wry face,the slap of the hand tears the papery skin from the crying face,old and grey with one foot in the grave;wear the purple habit to cleanse the soul,a freedom at last in the darkest hour before the rising of the watery sun in a new dawn of a day like yesterday,the tea pot simmers with a fresh brew wrangled from a green leaf blowing in the wind of change;the little girl kicking her frail legs on the swing,precariously dangling from the brittle branch of a rotten tree,ready to fall apart in the blue eyes of the little girl resigned to her imminent fate,staring at the fluffy clouds floating through the sky,stand tall and proud in the kiss of the red lips on the drained face of the little girl still living on the swing of the merry go round and round the rotten tree to smile at the crispy leaves falling all around her on the merry go round of life doesn't get much better;the bruised face cracks in a fake smile,waiting for the egregious laugh at your own joke,black and blue with a hint of pink,the dry skin of the red soaked lips bleed to stop the stabbing pain in the bulging nose,twisted in bated breath,take no pity on me,take no pity on you in a bout of self pity,cast away with no pity at all,a tender nibble on the delicate ear,lick the sweat on the flesh with a flicker of the rough tongue,stab a shivering flirt down her bony spine to tickle her most voluptuous desire;a cold slap on the pocked face stabbed in a spiky stubble;haggard over time to rest awhile on the cold slab,the rugged mind drained of all emotion,wishing you the best in the face of adversity to spite the vulnerable image tainted in the smashing mirror,no one will ever adore the ground you walk on in full stride to find your way on the hard road of the beaten path;day turns into the eerie darkness of the foggy night haunting you to the grave of another;the ghost of the monk will haunt you in his bed of golden straw,money reneged for his constant prayer,sleep with one eye open,bloodshot in fear of the ghostly monk on the rampage in the house of shame,flash a candle of hope   on the dim hallway,quietly make your escape into the promised land,where the brave are never free to run and hide in the shadow of light,the joker will always laugh in the face of integrity,the marbled staircase will destroy you in a sudden crumble to the ground where you were born in the spirit to survive the tempest of life;never look back at the hag witch with the spell wrapped o'er her stooped shoulder waiting to cast her evil net o'er the righteous innocent playing in the field of youth,the seed yet to be sown in a far away journey to the promised land,still a million miles away as the child sleeps in the swing hanging precariously from the rotten tree,watch the dead bird decay on the timber gate,allow it to fade away into its own mire without a touch from the pure hand,the evil stench will blow away in the cold wind of winter,the buds of spring will sprout new life into the dormant mind awoken by the warmth of the morning sun shining through window pane on the face of the sleeping child in a loving kiss from the beloved mother worked to the bone by the lazy man of the house;love will conquer hate in the end,throw caution to the wind that will take you afar one day,second to none to face the storm ahead,still dead calm in the lap of the gods to guide you with a holy hand on the pious heart, the fate of faith will banish the wrath of the gossip tongue,the evil words will burn forever in the flames of the eternal fire of the heart;knock and someone will open the door to take you away and save you from the hungry wolf of the wilderness,flashing the sharp fangs dripping in the blood of the meek;nature will take its course,a stark nakedness piercing through the glass eye blind in a shattered bewilderment of the beholder frightened of the shadow dancing in the dark corner of life;the clap of the thunder rumbles through the humid sky full in the power of rain waiting to fall down on the dust bowl,it never rains to wet the selfish appetite for the gaping neck to grow more slender in the passing of time to eventually take your breath away in the click of a broken finger,point the dirty finger at another but never at the image in the cracked mirror,a slave to your own madness,a burning fester about to explode in the mind to hit the fan at full speed in the pungent air of the mad stare into an empty void in a rush of blood to the head,snap yourself free in the pull yourself together before it's too late;the troubled child dressed in the image of the alpha male shackled in the chains of deceit,trampled in the glory of a slow demise in the face of humanity on the run to save the world;black on black,white on white,black on white,white on black,a firm handshake in the smile of a tender kiss in the darkest night to make it right,the word of peace to be written in stone bulging from the dirt of the fertile soil;the tryst full in the splendour of a manic lust,leaking in the tears of a painful regret,dry in the stain of a caustic fluid flowing into the cold stream;the gaping wound still a scar in the sad face of humanity,stray away into the onerous yelp of the mad dog on its last legs,profusely beaten by its master with an itchy hand on the bloodstained whip,others suffer at the hands of another's insanity on the run from the amiable reality,the easy way out for the evil brute is in the physical and mental desired force to destroy in all denial of a contemptuous rage on a ruled society at the mercy of bigoted fascists;a recurring dream full in the memory of hope drained from the growing mind where euphoria is denounced in the vicious slap of the clubhand,the mind saturated in the anger of violence,drag the frayed sleeve across the youthful nose to wipe the snot away in the flick of the green bones of the hand to land on the floor covered in the sawdust of a felled tree,cut down in the prime of life,dressed in the same old rags forever staring you in the resigned face;the caged children eventually leave to find themselves isolated in a place of no hope,sprayed in a desperation of a doomed failure,the dyke full in the splendour of a curdled poverty,branded on the rump of the shackled peasant, the philistines on the run with the hungry rats in the gutter of the ghetto,living life to the full in a perfumed sewer;the select political clown will run with the hare and hunt with the hounds to line their pockets in a sponsored donation of hush money to scatter dirty pebbles on the doorstep of the poor,never get caught with the greedy hand in the till,scratch the back with the long knives,dyed in the blood of slaves to the slaughter,count the gold in the bedroom of a shamed hysteria to eat with a silver spoon in the gaping mouth for the poor to scavenge on the animal scraps,cold and dirty in the rusty bowl of the gutter;the scraped fish scales drift away to settle on the sea floor,food for the tiny creatures of the abyss,the stardust to rest on the seventh day,flying high on the horsetail of the fluffy cloud floating across the sky;the glass half full in the emptiness of a the parched lips gagging for the wet kiss of love,greet the lost friend in a firm handshake to break free from the jealous secret stored in the back of the troubled mind,a flash in the pan,your goose is cooked in an embarrassed defeat,the log cabin in the woods for a rainy day has gone up in the flames of a choking smoke,where you will never grow old and grey in the passing of time;slurp on something hot in a glass of ice to wash the potent pill away,sat in the rocking chair drifting you into the sudden sleep of a fabled dream,taking the old man for a walk down memory lane,greeted by a stark naked surprise,grateful to be alive and kicking,watch the waterfall hit the cold stream in a splash of delight,the rumble of the rush blows o'er the deaf ear,take the old dog for a friendly walk on the soft path to sleep in the rocking chair with one eye open;mumble your life story to the stranger at the forest gate,when everything you touched turned to stone,but still alive and kicking in the sparkle of the glass eye,grey and old in the rocking chair of a hard life on the stomping ground of the forefathers,the dust scattered on the forest floor of moss,asleep for an eternity;the lamb to the slaughter bleats for the mother long gone,never to return to the glory of the good auld days lost to the stillness of the craggy mountain,stained in the green grass of many shades that once nourished the mother of the lamb to the slaughter,vanished in the mist hanging o'er the mountain,a soft day to sprinkle life on the soul,rest awhile in the squint of the eye to ponder on water under the bridge,no more standing in the cry of the hovering hawk about to strike the sharp talons into the heart of a frightened soul pushed o'er the edge of a rock solid stability;too young to die,too old to live,the body now stooped in a bent tiredness,a trickle of tears to wash the dirt from the wrinkles stuck to the bewildered face;the rolling waves of the bustling sea crash into the tangled water foaming at the mouth,the frantic flap of the seagull's wing o'er the crest of the white wave,swooping high and low in search of the life lost to the sea;the mercy cry of the seagull bouncing in an eerie echo through the massive roll of the breaker tumbling in a roaring dance on the bed of the sea floor,the giveth and the taketh of life as we know it in the spray of the divine salt in the body and blood of humanity;sleep until the morning sun shines on the tired body to warm the heart into a steady beat back to life in a lame survival to kick the jealous habit and pull yourself together in the clap of the slender hand;laugh in the face of shame on the bigot whose never wrong,a sociopath to destroy the glory for others living a righteous life;

a shyness so cruel on the child born to survive the wrath in the angry crowd of philistines,sleep with your back to the wall,kick the dust of retribution into the laughing face of the mocking people,blind to the talent of the painfully shy child,so afraid to commit in the release of the perfect talent,fly away on the wing of the celestial butterfly to land on a cloud of hope and love,live happy ever after in a fairytale story never to leave the ripe lips of a raconteur,lost to the folklore of a treasured culture;a misty condensation forms on the window pane,dirty in years of neglect to scratch a happy note on the glass with the rough skin of the skinny finger,twisted in a broken demise of the man struggling to write his own name,old Ted was here in the year of the great freeze,the ground rock solid in the graveyard,a warning for folk to stay alive in a firm right to survive your own birth;the good die young,so folk say with bated breath,that's if one is allowed to be born at all,slaughtered in the worm before the first cry of life,kill the innocent with a smile on the face of the ignorant possessed in the depraved mind,with blood flowing into the gutter of shame,the unmarked grave of the metaphorical cry for justice,a baby never given a chance to survive,to live on the milk of the beloved mother's breast;a second,a minute in the hour of the day turning into the week of the month,ending in the year with the most glorious birth of all time,cherish life not kill it dead in the womb of life before birth;silence is golden,listen to the silence,hear the silence,stare into the silence of regret cracked in the face of the mirror that never lies, a slap in the face of humanity,take the mask off before you die in the arms of your own shadow hiding in the dark corner;suck the goodness out of the leaking nipple,not the life out of a baby about to cry in the gulp of the first breath in the breaking of the water into the sea,a slave to life in death taking you to a better place;blame it all on someone else,never blame it on yourself,it's good to be alive in the face of adversity,time and time again,the pink flesh never to see the light of day in the love of a mother to blow a kiss your way,a lucky charm to protect you on the long,arduous journey through life in a foreign land,never to go back to the place of birth in the longest hour before the dawn;there's no point in crying over spilt milk gone sour in the water under the bridge,if and when the story ends,you have to do it all over again,like it or not with a weary smile on the sad face to greet another day of survival;strum on the sweet chord that will never play on the vinyl disc,the birds sing in a hoarse voice,a crackle in a cradle of lament,the birds don't sing anymore on the tree reaching out to the blue sky,the emotions of a struggling moment in time has saddened the birds to a secret hideaway,where humans are refused entry,all the money in the world will not save you in the end,take control of your own destiny before it's too late;enter the twilight zone in full flight to dazzle you blind as the flash of the violent light beams in a horrid terror on the people stranded in their own mire;the shadow play dances in anger,a clap of thunder rumbles through the dark sky full of rain and anger, the lightening crackling across the sky in a roaring anger,waiting to strike venom on to the land burning in a ring of fire through the tree of life;ride the crest of the wave in the sky hiding in the crack of a wise light,the funeral pyres are burning all in a row,the hovering smoke a signal to mankind;the sweet smoke of the clay pipe puffing through the lips of the old man leaning on the broken gate,the bloodshot eyes gazing o'er the land of his birth,the toil of the land still in his skinny,bony hands,now full in the pain of a hard life on the side of a mountain,the weary hand stuck to the stem of the clay pipe,a warmth to behold in the old age of a stooped man still in love with life,the crippled feet achingly warm in boots older than the mountain hanging on to the old man dragging himself back to his cosy cottage by the cold stream,relax the bones in the autumn of life by the open hearth fire roaring out in flames to warm the heart of the old man sipping on a bottle of porter,a frail freedom hanging on tender hooks as the day draws to an end in the bloodshot eyes of the old man asleep by the roaring fire,spitting sparks of love in the beauty sleep of a tired man,a raucous snore into the night;a brittle branch snaps o'er the mountain stream,cold as ice to tickle the roof of the old man asleep in the rocking chair of his treasured life on the mountain,the cold water of the stream slowly cuts a scar into the heart struggling to stay alive;the morning sun beams a ray of light to stoke the fire of the old man back to life,the simmering kettle,black as soot,hanging on a chimney hook,dripping boiling water into a mug of tea, a skelp of ham in the dirty hand for breakfast and out to milk the lonely cow into the bucket of its youth,a cold splash of water from the mountain stream to wash the face slippery as ice in the autumn of his life,the cold stream standing still to shade the trout feeding on the early worm,wriggling on the sandy bed as the old man splashes a fishing line into the stream to greet the hungry trout to strike on his rusty hook in a swooping leap from the water to land on the bank covered in the golden leaves of autumn,the pouting trout,dressed in the colour of the rainbow,slowly fades away to keep the old man alive for another day in his life on the mountain;the chirpy birds wash in the cold stream,singing to the old man naked in the water,splashing a rare kindness on the birds happy to share the stream with the old man,laughing himself stupid in a lame reminisce of his long life on the side of a glorious mountain,a fond farewell to the people of yore,now no more,but not forgotten;the good folk wrestle and sleep with the bad offered to them without dispute,take life as it comes your way,meet and greet it head-on in the face of adversity,the good will prevail in the end;the fall from grace will be great in the demise of the proclaimed narcissist,lost in a shroud of vanity on the run from reality,the big fish will eat away at the small fry burnt to a cinder,an open book that cannot be read in a penny for your thoughts my dear,the echo of life on the run from the people you trusted with your life,no more the bad man,no more the good man,in no more the man for all seasons,if for any season at all, read the words in the flicker of the glowing candle,all the money in the world won't make you happy,the grim reaper will suck the life out of the sleeping womb until death do us part in the scrape of the stiletto worn to the bone;the angels fly on pious wing,taking the soul of innocence to paradise,a silent revenge on the wicked hiding in the darkness,crying in the emotional crumble to stare into the face of a bitter silence,a shroud of guilt to stain the heart in the last gush of life,rubbing the integrity from the face of humanity in taking a bite out of the forbidden fruit still falling from the tree of life;eat and be eaten,banished into an aching blindness in the turmoil of living a life shackled in a shamed contempt,failing to scrub the iniquity away,far away into a distant land of mirage where life is hidden in the sand;salute or be blown away in the slap of the fat hand of a depraved teacher frothing at the mouth,screaming words of confusion on the cracked mirror of the pocked face,academia about to explode in a splatter of hate on the innocence with their hands tied in a black knot;the jam stained in the honey of the gravy swirling on the dirty plate,slurp it all away in a greedy gulp of a choking cough with tears in the eyes,alive to fight the madness of another day;woman up to the man who couldn't man up to the woman on the run from reality staring them naked in the gaping face,a hard slap on the truth of the water running hot and cold into the sinking hole,slippery in the stank wetness of a rat squealing in a cage;black power written on white paper slowly fading into a cream of delight in the denial of human rights, a muffled voice in a restrained muscle to stop the yelp in the shiver of the caged rat, no rest for the wicked mind of destruction; no sleep for the sheep huddled together in a corner of deserted land,contaminated in the filth of human waste dripping from the polluted pores of shining skin;ba ba for the black sheep of the family,long lost to the material world growing more greedy every day,sow the seed of love too old to grow in a shriveled fertility,a fluidity dripping in the image of a screaming squirt too young to die in the old age of a wrinkled potato pealed away in the raw flesh stale in the sweat of a tearful struggle;blow hard on the sonorous nose until the blood flows away in the sins of the hardened flesh;stone deaf to the sound of the soft voice in the aching ear blind to the sensitive touch of a consoling soul,touch the blank canvas dancing with the bouncing shadow,fading into the moonlit night,the squinting eyes strained in the focus on the dark specks of the troubled mind,stardust gushing through the gappy teeth so sexy in women and ugly in men,the cry for mercy in the dentist chair with tears of pain grinding away at the rotten teeth,milky and soft in the reluctant gappy smile,the dim light never lies to the blind eye with the fuzzy smile,blink and you miss it forever more in the kiss of the bad breath puffing in the sweet smoke of the clay pipe,everything in black and white has a colour tinge of blindness,the blank canvas,naked and ashamed of the blind mind itching to splash dirt on the rare image tearing through the disturbed mind of the failing artist scared of his own demise staring at him in the cracked mirror hanging precariously on the flaking wall of his crazed life;the starry night stuck to the blinking eyes weeping in the soft voice,the creaking door resting on the fresh grave,waiting patiently for the knock on heaven's door,leading to a fabled paradise trapped in a deluded hypocrisy,you will never be ready to meet your maker,people who believe they can see are really just the blind leading the blind up the garden path,rushing on a white knuckle ride without a paddle, only to crash into a sucking ferocious whirlpool of a brutal destruction,gulping a fond farewell on the cold water of strife;the door knocking noisily on the grave,a soft day thank God for another tomorrow,a tear of joy trickles down the hardened face,weary in the abuse of time, keep on knocking and the jammed door will eventually open wider than the free bird in the bluest sky of the dark night;walk on to the blank canvas in a gasp of breath to kiss the paint dry,the red lips bleed in a dripping paint,a wink of the blind eye to cry itself asleep in the middle of the night;the grass is wet but greener over there,the shoe is on the foot of the wrong person,without matching socks,add more fuel to the dying fire,a boom to the weak heart in the pious month of November,the heart pumps for you and me within,without in the heat of the smoking gun too hot to handle;the noisy stream ravaging down the side of the mountain in the melt of the winter's snow sparkling in the blue tinge of the ice,slippery on the tongue of the wild beast drinking on the coldness of time;the weak are strong in the dormant talent asleep for another year on the run from a stark reality,if you stumble and fall,bounce back stronger in the dirty face of adversity;the slippery snake wriggling o'er the bulging roots of the ancient tree,towering o'er the fluffy clouds of the warm sky,a warning to the snake to wriggle cautiously o'er the rough bark clinging to the mighty tree,where the little birds nest on a bed of crispy leaves,dressed in the soft feathers of a loving mother on the hunt for food,a sharp beak to stab the snake into a hissing submission,swirling to the floor to greet the roots with a mighty bang,slimy in defeat,the snake slowly stretches its aching body into a dark hole at the edge of the forest;a dystopian chill moves through the humid air on a land now ravaged by a virus disease coming to get you in the early morning of the late night,spreading an even more greedy mayhem on the human animals growing more beastly by the hour of the suffering day,the roof of life is falling down all around you and nobody can fix it in the old thatch of yore no more;the birth of a powerful wave swelling into a rolling intent of the eventual death staring you in the cold face of a certain fate splashed in your eyes from the early age of dawn,the secret buried in the golden sand of a deserted beach,the lonely soul floats away on a twist of driftwood on a windy day into the deep abyss,gravity will suck you into the wide,open sea in a boat without a sail,aimlessly drifting until judgment day for the lost soul asleep in the boat;swing high,swing low in the flaying arms punching through the heavy air only to tumble head over heels, bounce back even stronger to confront the laughing mad bully,the jealous aggressor dressed in the image of a deranged demon;drink yourself sober in the rising sun of a new dawn,flying high as a kite with the low flying birds feeding on scraps;caress the wig full of fake curls to roll into a soft ball for the cat to play with feathers flying all over the place,punching above your weight in a room plastered in blood money for the death of another,the old rope frayed and ready to snap in the sharp teeth of a mad dog starved and hungry for flesh dressed in the glad rags fit for a Queen on a King,cross-dressed in the cynical smile of the red lipstick blotched on the bulging lips bleeding for a deserved mercy on the terrified soul stripped naked in a room full of bulging eyes ready for the kill with a smile on the butchered face of a sardonic intent on the naked slave to the slaughter;a burst blood vessel gushing through the bulging lips of the wretched mouth crippled in the splatter of blood on the cracked mirror staring you boldly in the face;drink yourself sober time and time again,dragging the aching legs on the hard road leading you astray in the smack of the parched tongue on the fluttering lips stuck to the dirty glass of porter,drink yourself into an early grave where time ticks away on the clock of life waiting for no beast on the hunt of destruction;the bleeding sun sleeps behind the mountain steeped in the history of the forefathers hard as nails,scraping a living on the land,a barren place on the side of a mountain to soak it all inside on a soft day for the hardened folk worked to the brittle bone;

the rain taps on the window pane in a tender trickle of love on the eye looking through the stained glass,a scrape on the dirt lodged on the bottom of a green bottle,lost in the dirt of the weedy garden growing outside the window;crying in the pain of a thousand tears of the sad day lost in the sadness of the dark night,turning the stardust into a sparkling light across the starry sky in the prime of life,the sweetness is licked dry of all duress,never a mess in a strained strife on the run from the staring shadow;the silver spoon grown rusty in the golden mouth of privilege to form a wealth of flesh in the making,looking down on the poor soul sleeping in the gutter;too old to make the grade in the life of a wasted youth trapped in the warped spirit of a rat cage,the black rat spitting poison in the face of a human decay unto themselves;a stray dog chews on a naked bone that will never crumble like the flesh,the wheezing lungs snore in a gasping farewell to the lonely soul buried in the sweat of the creaking bed,the meek are never poor in the spirit of the mind blanched by the greed of the rich stuck in the eye of a needle lost in the dust of the haystack starting to rot in the seed of a shamed hatred;a dog barks in the distance,clapping in a fading echo as the master shouts abuse at the poor soul to hang high on a broken branch without any remorse at all,the dog is put out of its misery at long last going to a better place where the sun shines brightly on the light of the poor beast,now a tender,loving soul laughing through life;the loaded gun never to miss the huge target piercing through the middle of the blind eye that has seen it all before the flickering light of the candle flashed out in a gush of sodden air,kiss the stench in the trenches of a war so great in the slaughter of the innocent,lost in the command of a cretinous crew of educated fools locked away in a pristine mansion full of brandy and bulging cigars for the old chaps bored out of their wretched minds,stab the bayonet straight through the already sleeping heart in no man's land,a wet grave without a cause for the brave to the slaughter,the brandy soaks in the thick moustache puffing cigar smoke into the clouded air;the sad women throw a feather of shame on the wise man refusing to fight in a lost battle,hide behind a cowardly veil coated in the dirt of shame,too young to die in the old age of madness,the sauerkraut bleeding in a rawness in the fermented trenches without a cause,heavy handed on the trigger of death,the trenches flowing in a river of blood,the broken mind bleeds in a poem,a Sassoon huddled in the words of Owen at the end of a bloody day on the run from a mad reality punched into the mind of the brave soldier never to return home to the land of his birth,a headstone without a name when your number is up,you've got to go and meet your maker in a cry for mother;Haig and Kitchener,the great butchers of the war,brave men die in a puff of smoke,a betrayal to the masses in a riddle of foreign bullets;the bureaucrats still munch on the finest caviar to stain the silver spoon,washed down in a slug of brandy;the bird on light wing,swishing through the air on the hunt for the blind eye of command in the slaughter of the innocent gone stone mad on the gas of delirium floating o'er the open trenches of men fast asleep,never to be awoken by the tender kiss of a lover greeting a new dawn;kick the sanity into touch in a blinking hope of survival,take the boat to the edge of the ocean in the deep blue sea where the fish survive the lashing wrath of the raging water crashing on the rocks,the dead show more emotion in the corpse than the living skeleton in a state of shock,a bullet fired from a smoking gun at slow speed,returning to haunt the bewildered soul hiding in a shell shock mind forever more,the lost piece of the jig saw buried in the blast of the angry gun,the blotted face bouncing in the echo of the wandering mind jumping from the body,a splash of paint to dazzle the eye,aging old in the barrel of the smoking gun,sat on a nervous bed,drifting into a trembling sleep,the bang of the gun will disturb you no more,walk into a room full of insomnia,feel the blink of the eye wide open,glued to the eye brow,the grandfather's clock ticks away in the old age of youth laughing in the face of death,follow the others into the garden of life to while away the time in a moment of bliss;beware of the treacherous journey through the thick wood of the haunting forest waiting to take you away in a gush of wind,run in the shadow of the worn path and never look back on the ghostly past,shock the mind out of a crazy madness in a slow drip to resuscitate your life into a sane normality,sail through the forest in a sea of trees,never to miss the boat again in a strong breeze blowing through the bulging sails flapping in the wind of change;

no more the lunatic living life on the run beneath the crashing waves,sucking life out of the sand of the golden beach,grip firmly on the rope anchored in the deep explosion of the abyss,cry for no one,not even yourself,a shipwreck full of fallen stars dripping from the emotional sky;bite the bullet in the gobby mouth of the educated prigs dressed in the rags of legal thugs running with the greedy banker and hunting with the corrupt state scratching the dusty wigs of lost change,tax the poor to feed the rich gravy train speeding on a track of money for old rope;judge not to be judged by the blind leading the blind,the lobster sucking the life out of the crab clinging to the oyster hiding the dashing peril of the sea,nourished by the salt of the water,a rubber stamp on the rump of life with an itch that cannot be scratched without lashings of blood squirting into your painted face,cover it all over in a tainted mask ready to be cracked in the heat of the moment,a secret never to be revealed to the crazed mass of celebrated delinquents shackled to the tag of celebrity,zapped in a fusion of addiction,don't you know who I am when I paint by numbers, even when there's no paint;anything can happen when you dream in the middle of the subconscious night,scream with the mouth wide shut,the bleeding stuck to the roof of the mouth,a reality in real time to drink yourself sober in front of a judge,coated in a redness to beat the band on the run with no money,cold as ice in the hidden iceberg,blue in the face of the arctic bliss in the look of love,the raw flesh sucking life out of death sleeping in a wooden box of six inch nails;

a bipolar reaction in the mind of all minds,black dots dancing o'er the eyes,blinking in a scarred bloodshot sliding down the long nose slowly fading away from the face;sleeping in the deathbed of another,the shriveled mouth wide open in a laughing scream jumping out in strange words mumbled through the gappy teeth,hold a sea shell to the deaf ear to hear again through the echo of the clapping ocean,a war to end all wars blasted in the hatred of other people growling like mad dogs,starving in the chase of their own tail;splash paint on the canvas of your life,black in the colour of white,a fuzzy beard to cover the gaping scare on the face slashed by the evil of another's insanity,a state of the warped cloud hanging o'er the polluted air we breathe to stay alive and kicking to die,but not before the last drink from the empty cup full of dust under a scabby crust;a caged bird flapping for a deserved freedom,a caged human gone mad hoping for it to end,a caged rat squealing through the rusty bars,we are all trapped in some kind of a cage,send you away with a special brew to help you sleep in the art of rocking you awake in the cry of the morning,hammer until you can't hammer no more in the echo of the mind flying around the empty room,depressed in a dreary boredom of failure,a resigned darkness in a sunny day full of rain,a punch in the eye to turn black and blue in a hue of a pink clot to never leave the face;the buttocks slim in a slight beguiling flash in the squinting eye,a feline scratch of the piercing claws on the delicate flesh so soft,softer than the most alluring nude in the night, on the run from time herself,a voluptuous wretch falling apart at the frayed seams,a courtesan hiding in the arms of the wealthy lover burning in the sin of lust bursting through the decaying veins about to explode for the last time,die happy to die at all in the sun drenched arms of the smiling courtesan bulging in the wealth of the vanished lover;the tramlines will crumble under the foot of the red stiletto digging deep into the tortured mind of the lost soul,scraping a life out of the metal tracks;scribble your warped thoughts on a black and white newspaper full in the words of the aching heart,a jealous heart on the hunt to persuade in the manipulation of the ignorant mind afraid of the simplest committal of elementary deduction,the power of the chosen few prevails in the ghetto of the struggling peasants too nervous to sleep with the squealing rats trapped in the concrete cage;pull the wool o'er the sore eyes soaked in the stale blood of the damned,if you struggle to control your own mind,then how can you seduce the dried juices of a potential lover teasing your confidence away into the bowels of a flirtatious ghoul,an infantile trait stuck to the wrinkled brow of old age;draw your life away in the stroke of a feathered brush barren of words written from the heart,wander aimlessly through the park trodden to the bone,bare of flesh and life in any shade of green to enlighten the tired eyes confused into a blind blink of delirium;the ballerina struggling to dance on a broken toe to the screams of her demented teacher staring deep into the cracked mirror hanging on the crumbling wall of the ballerina's soul,the art dripping through the painted mind,deeply censored in the perverted states,corrupt in the ideology of slavery on a nation stifled by the madness of a dictator in love with himself;sex on the run invented for the old but shagged by the young waiting to slaughter the unborn soul in a sacrificial clot to the brain;know your place or be whipped into a painful submission,the flesh will melt on the bone about to snap in two,a stroke to the state of mind soon to be a vicious victim of the political enemy,a slow death shackled to the damp wall of a prison cell,a home from home,the temptation of Eve is coming back to haunt you so in love with yourself;the croaking frog will spawn all o'er the precious fresco fading away on the ancient wall about to fall,cry out for mercy for the last time of your decrepit existence in a land stranger than the strange loner lost to the power of survival,release the monster dormant in the broken heart crying out in a shamed delirium,pull yourself back into the dark hole of a planned birth gone wrong,granny will lowly forgive your ignorance in a chastised slap in the cold face laughing on a shining light glowing for everyone,someone like you,a calamity simmering on the fire spitting sparks on a strained humanity;go west to save your soul in the going down of the sun,this land belongs to the brave but not the free,the whole truth and nothing but the truth,not in the best of my knowledge or my recollection fails me with the hand on the pious book,a bloody damnation on the prig not fit for purpose,a mangy dog lost on the road;

nobody knows me,but I know myself,living it up at the hotel of life where you can check out anytime you like but you can never leave,you've lost it all,but gained everything in the clap of a cold hand,the echo of life staring you in the face,the empty space is still there regardless of the pending blues humming on a metal string,you are dead in the head,let the sun beat a burning desire in the face,climb the highest mountain made of rock,do,du,do do,du,do,if I hear you cry,I'll be back to haunt you to the grave hidden in the graveyard,the vehicle breaks down as you mind goes on the blink for the last time,never dream again about the good times gone bad,you now cannot even read between the dark lines scribbled in a blind whiteness to wet the blank page with ink,astute in a complacent sharpness slashing out in the flaying arm about to fall off in the gentlest touch,a gush of wind blowing through the slashed sail,hone your skills to slip it in only for it to slip out twice as quick in the howling laugh of a deluded thespian,afraid to stare into the mirror of a cracked life,soaked in a pungent sponge floating in a bucket of dirty water,leaking at the bottom to drain the dirt from the water in the drying of the sponge gone hard as a rock,the salt of the water eats away at the dying sponge,the aftermath of the hardened sponge in the head of the old man leaning on the broken gate about to vanish into the haze floating o'er the old man full in the tears of a terrible illusion squeezing hard on the long throat in the suffocation of the wave gushing through the gaping mouth;a crazy harshness cracking on the lips of the haggard head hiding in the black shawl,the harlequin of colour fading in the dark mind;stretch the cramp leg to ease the excruciating pain,a radical approach for the medication taken from the doctor's bag,the slow death of drugs keeping you alive to live just another day,five,ten,fifteen a day,take your pick in a slurp of tepid water dripping from the leaking tap,go to bed to sleep the drugs away in the start of a new dawn beaming through the moonlit night;the radiant mind of the subdued child thwarted in the laugh of the jealous evil growing larger than life on the barnacle of a blown trumpet,stuck to the lips of the hypocritical bigot scared of his own shadow,raging a roaring contempt on the talent of another precocious star born to fail in the eyes of the glory boys dressed as girls gagging for more of the same,don't dally around the room of shame where nobody sane can procreate in the lost orgasm of a wasted youth in the sweat of the dry orifice,a virgin at birth until the death of a depraved satisfaction;grow old gracefully not in the jealous shame of another trying to live the life of a fallen star,staring them in the wrinkled face slashed of all dignity,better to be celibate than live a life like you,the hot wax will tear the skin away,leaving the hairy pubes in tact to be stroked by the sticky fingers,licked back to life by the dry tongue raging like a mad dog;look away before it's too late,but never look back into the abyss that will suck your mind senseless,a postcard for a forgotten birth,scattered in the wilted petals of a surging flower ready to pollinate all over again and again, just like the wild animal trapped in the savage human, an innate flagellation sizzling in the loins of dust blown away in the howling wind of the crying nigh full in the rage of a cracking storm;go now to let go of all the bad times turned good in the depressed mind of a ravaged despair,keep it away by shouting at it in the daylight of the insomnia staring at the strange night, have a private moment,sat high on the bed,deprived of the huge amount of sleep blinking through the blind eye,void of any kind of emotion pumping in the heart of a coldness afraid of the heat in the beat of the shivering finger,the long finger bent in a broken pain aching through the smashed hand,tired;the young lad to pick up the prize for winning the race in a barren field of other young lads all racing towards the finish line painted white for the little cup,smeared in a tainted silver,cheap but still nice for the young lad to place on the old mantle piece where granny had the black elephant full of money for food and coal to sleep in the roaring fire,ready and waiting for the tobacco stained saliva granddad clearing the phlegm from his coughing throat,the phlegm sizzling on the fireplace grate,leaving a messy stain in the heat of the moment to last a little bit longer,the old hand lightly smacks the clay pipe on the grate to free it of the hardened ash climbing up the sooty chimney,blown away into the early evening light,sat deep in the worn armchair rocking the old man asleep to the lullaby of the spitting sparks landing on the linoleum floor,pocked in the skin of youth,the blazing fire takes care of the old man snoring in the worn armchair that once belonged to the grumpy father full in the anger of porter,the beauty of his lost love glows in the dancing flames of the roaring fire;we'll meet again where the smiling words never dare to progress into a stark reality of a cuddled embrace turning into the erotic kiss of lovers soon to be senseless lovebirds locked in the juices of a prolonged lust;the sore eyes of the old man squint into the fire waiting to be stoked by the black porker,a piece of metal to tap on the heated grate burning in a desired freedom,the devil you know is better than the devil waiting to take the bit out of the hungry mouth, the flames will warm the soul to the grave waiting to be dug by the old hand that once shook the world ,but no more able to close in a tight grip on reality;the bottom of the top is waiting to suck you into the hole forever more in a ritual to finish you off in an instant click of the hardened finger,so crude in a refined rudeness;the message of truth is painted on the flaking wall,a slow fade away into a loving oblivion staring you in the blank face;the derelict cottage wall stands proudly tall,with the name of youth scratched deep into the damp plaster,hanging on the rough stone like wallpaper without the paste,the snap of an outstretched branch dangling on a rotten beam spitting a dusty powder on the floor covered in the weed of the wild flowers of the mountain,the misty rain of yore still sleeps on the iron headboard of the vanished bed,the aching spine still coiled around the rusty springs of the sodden mattress,a cherished haven for the crippled bones of the old man puffing on his clay pipe,a sweet smoke to float o'er the valley, the yellow hay tangled in the sprouting grass soaked to the skin in the summer of rain,the sooty kettle simmers on the crooked hook o'er the hearth of the open fire,the kindled sticks making a crackling noise to sooth the mind into a happy existence of isolation on the mountain,waiting to say farewell to the old man sat by the open hearth fire,smoking on his beloved clay pipe,hand paint the letter you'll never write on a slate hidden in the stonewall,the noisy neighbour home from the pub drunk and merry for another swig from the glass jug,a stabbing roar to ease the pain of the delirium shackled to the mind,cry not for yourself,but for another decrepit soul,howling in the echo of the cutting wind;talk to the man lost in the woman on the run from the abuse staring her in the crying face,the war paint streaming down her wrinkled face;swallow a jagged tablet washed down in the noisy slug of moonshine from the glass jug,hide the money with the sins soaked into the wall of the mountain,older than life itself;diamond and pearls are made under enormous pressure,some humans excel under the enormous pressure flashed before their eyes blinking in the scorching sun,beaming a pressure on the tender skin of life,run into the sunset in search of the elusive fame denied to most creatures of habit roaming the land without a cause,cry not for the failure of life,but cry for a wasted life,the sucker punch will get you in the end,bending you over to screw you for good measure;keep one eye open for the coward hiding in the shadow waiting to strike a killing blow in the jealous intent of wanting it all, the want of taking all is beaten into the mind by the devious cry of another sharing an empty space for life,the cream will always float to the top;the mad bear with a sore head becomes the intoxication of the mind drifting into a ravage bitterness fighting the anger into a screaming lunatic in what it feels like to be a jealous beggar on the hunt for a soothing sanity to free the mind of all bitterness;hold the anger high as a kite,like the gobby mouth fails to hold their whisht,spreading a hatred all over the stinking place,smash your own sculpture out of a cold slab of marble,holding your fine head high into the floating clouds of the bluest sky,you may fall and stumble out of the sculpture,but always return to the bursting water of the painful birth for mother and child;marry for the love in the name of another or refrain forever more,be prepared to die in the flick of a switch hanging o'er the deathbed soaked in the sweat of a hard life on the run from the apparition in the corner of the room,waiting to take you away to a better place in the next life,shake yourself senseless to find the ounce of sense,hold on because everything has a hold on something real in a masquerading way,blink and it's all over in a second,dead as a door nail,twisted and rusty and about to snap you into another life;run with the hare and hunt with the madness,a nervous reaction to a bigoted hypocrite,rubbing their hands in glee with the honourable distinction of a winner on the march for more glory won by another,live to deny the retched soul of a good life in the ghetto,a slumdog to lick the pus from the raw flesh leaving the bone;

wash yourself in dirty water to cleanse the soul,the fish starving in the frozen pond,full in the rainbow of the sky,crying in the acid rain in a slow burn on the planet;red shoes are never worn flat,always with a six inch nailed stiletto dragged bare to the worn tip,scraping at the frilly bra holding it all together,it's way too late for a cherished goodbye,the new viper is at the hand,devoid of all shame in the vibrator standing on the bedside table covered in the dust of a lost lust,the man in the sinking boat can row without a paddle but cannot swim into the orgasmic ecstasy,the branded image of the sinking boat will ride on the crest of the powerful wave,foaming a smile at the blue sky,a star to guide you through the darkest hour before the dawn of a new day,row,row and a row across the birth of a new sky raging in a flaming fire, the red tattoo stuck like dirt to the long arm,the skin rosy in a shiny paint,never wash away into the deep pool of a cold stream,a still life in water,a hideaway for the pouting fish in a smack of lipstick;if you see me,I can see you,if you stare at me,I can stare at you, if you look at me,I can look at you,look away now before it's too late for the woman in the man of the woman to survive the wrath of the dormant mind on the blink for the very last time,the best of times will never return,appear as normal,let's not squander a life away in the waffle of others stifled in their own mire of a profound indignant wryness on the boil too long,put an end to it now,once and for all,a distortion of the deranged mind in a freud of bacon burning in the dark pan,inhibit me to inhibit yourself in a moment of sarcasm,a silent recollection of a reel realness in the feelings and the sensations of the aesthetic slashed in the face of abstract expression for people to stare with a wide mouth open in the flashing of teeth on the rigid subject;woman rages against man,as man rages against himself in the image of a woman,return to the egg and start all over again,man loves woman in the love of a woman for a man,not just for juicy bits of stale semblance of the real thing,too late when the couple are limp and bone dry for it to happen all over again and again and again in a late discovery of flesh on flesh and bone on bone,only for it all to be a phony blank,when you desire to be moved,it's way too late as the curtain comes down o'er the stage,a slow leak to bring the ceiling down on the rigours of life,a musty blast of air floating o'er the empty room once full of life in the sound of happy children playing hide and seek a friend who cannot be found,a longing for a failed love in the chance of a fabled love locking horns with a fantasy lust,a slap in the blood starved face in the forbidden sunshine of a renounced love,only to start all over again with nothing but a shred of a starved illusion of grandeur,the poem that can never be finished in the stroke of a stubble brush digging into the broken heart,the haunt in the stamp of the scraping footsteps ripping through the soul,a disturbed delirium to flash through the warped mind,open the heart to feed the starved denial of a cumbersome cry for the naked muse running wild in the maze of the dense forest,the eye almost explodes in a weeping bulge of crocodile tears snapping at the limping heels brittle to the bone;the paint never dries in the mind to be well oiled,the bristle stuck to the brush will eventually fade away into the sunset at the end of the horizon,sleeping in the memory of the paint that once splashed on the blank canvas to a raving, ranting applause,create in the colours,a drip from the past,the ebb and flow of the humdrum way of a sustained denial,cherish the land painted by the sun in the idyllic image on the blank canvas,screaming for a splash of paint to ease the mind,the illusion of the abstract gesture dripping from the sky on the brush in a kiss on the canvas to paint a roof for humanity to live in a peaceful survival;old and decrepit but still going strong in the drag of the walking stick on the last leg home,a mushroom to spring into the night with a lashing of morning dew to wet the parched soul back to life,if only for a wet day of the starry night,longed to be loved much too much in the skip of a heartbeat in the aching chest,the perfect conscious of the subconscious asleep in the day of the night,way too late before you realize the mistake;the beauty of words on white paper in the beauty of paint on a blank canvas still rough and tough to the touch,watered down with a hint of paranoia to kick the mind into life,a lie in the stroke of a sham on the bristle of a ragged brush,the menace of the mind about to attack the canvas gagging to rage long into the light of a crazy new dawn,a strange beginning never to end in the point of the long tooth still attached to the third eye,the papery skin sticks to the frying pan sizzling on the open hearth fire,eat a skelp of bacon out of the fat of the hand;the mind will sketch a ghostly setting of the sun going down in the far away horizon,a romantic romance gone wrong in a muffled shuffle,a twist in the swing of the whipping tale of the mad dog running around in circles,depict the scene from a height to launch in a vertigo roll to crash the emotions on the slippery rocks,a slate sliding on the roof of the ancient cottage,tumble into the sand dune digging deep into the most arid desert floating into a vast serenity o'er the burning sand,search for the secret in the empty box of the doomed diva to fly away into the night sky with the wild birds of paradise;wearily tired of the big city and nervous of the country mile getting longer in a good morning turning into a bad day,getting better in the going down of the scorching sun;the moss spores spring into the forest,brother and sister in arms,running through the wood of the forest dense with red trees,older than the mountain;the evil that men do unto fellow men and women in the act of senseless wars on humanity,the violent atrocities of a determined bloodshed,the indiscriminate rape and slaughter of innocent women begging for mercy; a precious dynasty lost in the evil regime of mass destruction in the tender face of humanity by the dictators smiling in the cracked mirror,eventually to slide off the shifting plates changing the landscape of the world at war,a fragile reminder hidden in the crust of destruction,a loose grasp on reality;a red berry fusion to save the soul,hold to the lips to wet the parched throat in a kiss on the dry tongue of a fabled dream,wet and rosy trapped in the scrotum of youth to be carried far away in the barren landscape of a desperate isolation without a cause in full sight of the flickering lights on the blink;slide on the shine of the stair banister from the top of the top to the darkness of the bottomless pit in a never ending helter skelter rumbling in the raging mind,a sorry end to a privileged life with the silver spoon coated in a poisonous rust,the bestest friend is slowly going stone mad in the holding of a weak handshake,linking each other in the sanity of a paranoid insanity of schizophrenia running with the hare to fight the hounds into a barking submission gone wild;come fly away with me to the perfect place where life is wrapped in a naked bliss,a booze on a muse,if only for a muse lost in the strange stare of a total eclipse of the mind away with the fairies streaking across the misty mountain,follow the bright star of the dark night into a saving guidance;the sawn wood of the oldest tree will return to haunt the aggressor into a sawdust grave,the sore eyes cannot endure the blazed abuse any more,run only to be followed into the mass crowd of destruction,the black sheep of the family,the lost sheep of the family in the last shepherd of the family,all on the run from the someone of something,a mankind on the brink of extinction in the melt of the ice flowing into the sea,a makeshift life hanging on a frayed string shivering in the wind of an evil change frozen in the string;the blunt blade once cold in the scalper,now razor sharp to cut deep into the sensitive wick,dig deep into the soft flesh,weeping inexorable elegant in the drag of the aching bones to the end of the line,the moving picture of the Somme on the fateful morning of the brave men to the slaughter,cut down in the prime of life by the bullets of the raging machine gun steaming in the heat of death,even the blades of grass wilted and withered away into a stain on humanity,if the bullets fail to get you,the barbed wire will bleed you dry of sanity in a carpet of fire still blazing in the going down of the weeping sun,a loving silhouette to the dead,snared in the razor sharp barbed wire still tangled in the screaming mind;war played against war in the slaughter of millions through the blast of the bomb in the smoking gun of a stark lunacy on the run from a certain death,the requiem echoes in the stillness of the Abbey for the unknown warrior,people pass the grave with heads lowered in shame,a tear of forgiveness for the sins of war,a never ending war in a world slowly burning itself into the path of the Second Coming,shovel the dirt away with the arms broken in the pain of a thousand deaths sown in the red poppy fields,where the blood of the innocent brave once soaked the land to feed the poppy back to life,a penny for your thoughts my dear in the eyes of the faithful departed,the headstones so pristine,standing tall in a row for the dignitaries to smile in the munch of caviar awash in the bubbles of a fine champagne;dark in the decay of the flesh splashed in the submissive mind,full in a sexual delusion,a derision in a smack to the strained face limping in a mocking smile,the howling wind spitting in a furious anger on the sinners refusing to repent;the lone wolf snarling in the snap of the bloodied teeth, drink the sorrow away in the drug of a certain doom to stare into a stale glass of beer,the tormented mind contorted in a bed of sweat in the madhouse dreams of rats and snakes slithering o'er the aching body trapped in a decaying bed,greet a new dawn in a blasting roar from the shrinking throat,leap out of the stinking bed to drink another day into the starry night of a slow demise,a half empty glass full to the brim with the demon drink,scared to be taken away in the flush of the China storm killing people like flies falling from the sky,the sign of the times,the bomb to end all bombs in a changing future,the fierce melting of the flesh burning in the land of the fading sun;it may never happen to you,but be afraid to stare at the bruised mirror hanging on the crumbling wall,sleep through the dream of all dreams stuck to the blanket of a cold bed,taking you all the way to the other side in a boat full of sorrow;shiver in the shaking leaf flying around in circles to land on the tree of life blasted by the acid rain lashing out to crash land on the forsaken lawn,yellow in the sun burning red in the fury of the damned lost to humanity;the children are all alone to fend for themselves,the child leaf will grow strong into a crispy leaf to face the pain head-on into a stonewall;isolated in a shallow graveyard ,a brave solitude to endure for the last time in a shadow fight in front of the cracked mirror,stumble and it's all over for sure in the face drained of blood,holding the bony hands with the sweetheart straight from the fire of dreams about to explode in the face of a certain triumph,a delayed reaction a fabled desire;

the wrath of the violent storm will blow you away into a strange place at the end of the tunnel,the flickering light will lead you astray into a false pretense,enjoy life as long as you can in the spirit of honour;the mad scream will save you in the end,the smile remains in the face of the corpse,the people hanging on to the coffin are the saddest of the sad,waiting for the moment when it's too late,all alone in the morgue of your own demise,wandering aimlessly through life in the face of birth,you cannot put your broken finger on it in the end,the dirt trapped under the fingernails stick like jam to a crust of bread,naked to the very end,insomnia in the bed of the grave for the rest of your life,enjoy life for as long as you can,sleep on the hardened floor of the metal bed,the perfect moment never arrives on time,always too late in the pouring rain;the steam of the mist will rise to greet the dawn of the early morning,a gentle massage on the dirt of the worn path;be a man in the woman of the confused child,frightened of the dark in the room without a guiding light to console the mind into a deep sleep on a sheet of silk,drift into a copious dream of waves foaming at the mouth in a roaring crash on the golden sand of a rich tomorrow,money for nothing to live a glorious life in a treasured vista,blink and you will never find your way home,blinded by the light and the greedy emotions of grandeur in a cry of lament for more power to the people rolling in the claim of an indulged authority of a chiseled supremacy,vicious on the road to victory;the shattering shock of a blast to the brain in a mumbled rumble, the mind beset in a blood clot on the rampage in the feeble brain,ready to explode at the precise moment in a measured time,a delicate fusion of flesh and blood on the bone,the stoked fire about to bellow into a rumble of flames stripping you naked in the flash of the white teeth;a strapping girl walking into the blinding sun blinking o'er the eyes so sore in the flicker of the black spots driving you stone mad as a hare fighting in the frozen air,people laugh at you falling down the steep stairs in the snap of the fragile neck;the squealing pig's still alive but not kicking the hairy legs into the stank air,there in the mind and burning spirit of the bird of prey in full flight,on the hunt for the lost soul,the exposed talons lashing out to dig into the cold heart,a sudden beat to chime in the tick-tock of the grandfather's clock,gathering dust in the corner of the empty room,hiding in the shadow of the sun going down for the night of a new dawn soon to be born,the echo of the yelping dog lingers in the distance,heading for the edge of the mighty cliff hanging o'er the crashing wave longing to suck you into the deep abyss of a forgotten memory to fade away into the mist of the salty air;over the top to face your fate in the hissing bullet through the bleeding air, branded in your name,fall with the busted head in a spin,round and round in a farewell laughter for mother to kiss it better,the beloved mother's far away in another land praying for her baby to come home,life's a mirage in another's desire of how you should live your sorry life to the end in the name of honour,hang on in there for as long as you can to kick your crumbled can all over the place to fly full circle and return home old and dreary to the empty room of your birth,full in the dust of old age on the rampage for the last time,touch the velvet of the silk purse in a gentle caress of the long finger twisted in an aching demise; the bird of paradise pulsating in the colours of love to stretch the broken wing high and wide in a flight of fancy,never to kiss the fluffy clouds of the blue sky and glide with the wild wind taking you o'er the neverland of your dreams,a floating wish never to come true in the clip of the colourful wings flapping for a kiss;it's raining down on the sinking house,where once the good folk survived the wrath of the sizzling sun,no more the land of plenty,all soggy and wet in the corrupt state burning the money of the people starving on the last legs;the young old before their time,watching the walls fall down,soon to rise again in the mushroom of a bitter fight,take the talk to the end of the grueling walk on the hard road that killed the old dog with a smile on the evil face;the black crows fly home to roost in the nest touching the twilight sky to feed the starving child back to the land of the living where only the brave survive in the strength of an honourable strife,fly high with the cawing seagull on a delicate wing,hide the webbed feet in the warmth of the white feathers,hover o'er the rolling waves in the sea of life;the silk purse now well fingered by the twisted finger soaking in all the juices gushing like a waterfall on the wrinkled skin,moist as the morning dew awash on the wild flowers staying alive for the moment to meet the secret,darkness will always follow the brightest light streaking through the starry sky;the fruit cake rich in the stale porter ready for the big fight lasting to the bitter end for the last man standing in front of the laughing mirror,spit the broken teeth away,spit the blood to gurgle on the troubled mirror swinging on the crumbling wall,the wallpaper asleep on the wooden floor covered in the dust of dirt, stay in the house with a moss roof o'er the muddled head,fall into the arms of the four walls to dance the night away,stamp on the floor covered in the sawdust of the fallen tree,a snapping crash on the hard path to block the prancing stallion in search of the perfumed mare,broody in a resigned patience to meet her fate in the child bearing hips to tease her randy aggressor after only one thing,take it,have it,leave it,bugger off to sniff out another on the run from having a good time;lurking in the shadow of the dark alley wet in the rain of the soft day,tall in the skinny disguise of a man possessed in the beating drum of the jazz player, blowing loudly down the golden neck of a saxophone trapped in a glorious voice,the music rifles through the warm air of the chill night into an eerie silence,the empty bottle full to the brim in the dancing mind almost on the brink of madness,the saliva leaking through the bulging lips stuck on the roaring saxophone blowing in the mind of the jazz man,mad in the madness of the madhouse crying out for more jazz,sleep in the sweaty bed with the saxophone close to the heartbeat of the jazz still playing in your head,muted in the gurgling snore of the dry throat gasping for the stifled talent to shine like a diamond, run with wind on the bony spine to blow you into a celebrated lunatic;life is sprinkled with salt and pepper for someone else to devour in lashings of spicy intent, roots digging deep into the lifeless soil,suspicious that it will ever grow into the alluring man on the brink of a perfect life;the sea of sand growing day by day in the deadly desert of the vast Sahara,ride the hump of the camel through the endless dunes taking you to the city of gold,the Timbuktu of the desert,the ancestors buried in a grain of sand burning in the bones of the lost manuscripts,the white camel drinks at the rich oasis in the sand storm of the Tuareg turning into a sacred dust,the turban of the man runs deep in the veil of the woman's caress in the love of the sand to wander under the guiding star,the bright light of the desert;living in a refined seclusion on your own island,in your own castle,all alone to stare into the cobweb of your own oblivion,the inoperable tumour eats away at the sanity in the survival of the brave hanging on to a grave hope,a silent prayer to console the fragile mind back to life in the land of the living, the intellectual impulse is on the mend,at high speed on the bend to stay on the hard road of life,love yourself to love another on the perch of life,talk to each other about the insecurity of sleeping on the job, say hello to the struggling artist,a house painter on the mend in the abstract impression on the wall;the show off chip off the block,so good that he cut off all of his fat fingers,bang on the counter in the delirium of a madman clutching at a rare sanity,show some emotion in a cry for help,cry into your pint glass of stale beer,so stank that you cannot drink for your failing health,never mind that of a stranger sat beside you on a park bench,wet to the skin of the lost soul,it all seems to come together in the end of the dark tunnel,waiting for the light to shine in a glimmer of hope,the illusions eat away at the heart,the best of times lost in the worst of times beating in the lashing rain on the window pane,if you don't like me,how am I suppose to love you in a bile waiting to burst its pus all over the place,unravel in your own mire,wallow in your own filth,sleep in another's bed,wrestle with the demons on the dark side of a paranoid moment,the voices are bad in a good way,taking you to a strange space,walk your way through life in a daze on the run from reality,shackled to a cocoon,touch yourself when no one else will touch you with a barge pole,the mind of the wondrous spontaneity of impulse dashing through the eye,you can have everything and still have nothing at all;a hellish day for a child makes you sad,embrace adversity with a smile on the stern face, carry your cross well into the next life,face to face,rub nose to nose in the pout of the red lips,with a tongue shake for good measure,a bondage for life,walk away only to make a swift return to your birth, something happens to everything for a reason,people agree to disagree,regardless of knowledge when the voiceless rumblings of the heart spin out of control in whatever it take for success,soar higher and higher to gain more power,the fierce outrage in the return of the boat void of life;in my eyes,in your eyes,in the glass eye,in the eye of mankind,the atmosphere is blowing away in a changing forever,bad as bad can be in the half naked baked mind on the brink of another disaster that could have been avoided;run a country mile from having a good time in the frilly boudoir of her dreams, fall on the blunt sword to sharpen it into a deadly weapon of your choice,delusions of grandeur in the boring boudoir where the bed springs slowly rust in a snoring sleep into the night of the long day,the sweaty handshake of the chubby embrace,sniff it out,smoke it out,blow it all away in the puff of the rosy cheeks,soft in the grey stubble of old age creeping up on the wrinkled face,the brittle bones with one foot in the grave,when you're gone,you're gone for good,life goes on,on,on,on,on,on,on,on,on,on,on,on,on,on,on,on,on; let it be so for everyone yet to be born;washed up,the pounding of the rock over time by the angry water going mad with the natural hammer on the cliff face,the softness splashing into the sea foaming at the mouth like a wild animal on the hunt for blood,the sea stacks survive,standing tall in the salt of the sea,proud to be cleansed in the tidal bliss of the moon,adoringly saving the sea full of life,gushing in the bubbles bursting into a new birth,slapping life into the darkest abyss,the painting of sea stacks by the salt of the sea, white in the foam of the jiving wave hissing at the towering rock,standing all alone in the water rumbling in the anger of the staring moon,far away across the universe,the seas are controlled by a planetary force, benign to humanity,gravity will tear you apart in the echo of the clapping hand;talk to yourself and the voice will prevail,men come,women go,vanish into thin air to scream a fury at the starry night,eager in the lookout for more,lots more,rubbing shoulder to shoulder with the people of influence,leaving a vapour trail scar in the dark sky of your mind,never knowingly going on the blink,often on the drink to ease the pain tearing through the soul soon to be on another bumpy journey in a desperate move to a strange place,leave the land you've only ever known to sail away on your own into a private space,a place for love not war,high in the nest of a fluffy cloud,the frilly feathers of the night bird flaps to tickle the soul bouncing o'er the clouds full in the enthusiasm of a new life,no more slightly mad in a stone crazed delirium of a man gone mad in the head of a deranged woman still the fairest of them all,never let it be said your beloved mother reared a waster,a loser too lazy to wash away the self pity of the sore eyes bleeding in a blind rage to hide away in a dark place,a room without windows to shine a light on life,the windows outside draped in dusty curtains hanging high from a hook in the bluest sky;the ordeal will one day come to an end,the big bang will soon be a big bang again;search widely to find the secret,but will you ever find yourself wandering in the lonely night,hold a grudge and have a grudge float o'er your head forever more,take it to the graveyard,a misty fog to blind the already lost mind;run away with the beautiful child hot from the warm breast full in the milk of strife,a powerful wisdom to bleed the mind back to life,if only for a slight moment,break into a new beginning,the old background erased from the vast memory tainted, bring back time when the good old days were the best of times,bring back the birch to control the madness hanging on the edge of sanity,an insanity on the blink,a short wink of sleep,the alarm that never bleeps to greet the morning sun to start the working day;a Gorky back to life in a splash of colour on the painted face in the shape of the future,a surreal impression on the abstract mind,the best friend is the most jealous one to keep a glass eye dry in the tears of a regretful shame,the correct direction is not forthcoming from the trusted friend hiding in the wolf of the dead sheep, go now before it's too late in the day of the dark night on the run from the perfect eclipse of the mind,what do you see when you paint in a vibrant life,what do you see when you scribble words to possess the heart in the sound of a strummed chord,the power in the warped influence of the static mind always on the blink in a renounced denial of the stark reality staring you boldly in the scarred face,nature will take its course,pulling you this way,dragging you that way,to nowhere in the end of it all going wrong,but where did it all go wrong in the throw of caution to the wildest wind of change,black dripping into white in a brush of greyness,red is the colour of the confused mind in the blood of red,the raw flesh is alive in the redness of life,a comfort to behold in the palm of the hand full in the red paint of a cautious existence,stop the flickering lights in the colour of red,glow into the staring eyes waiting for the green light that never appears in the survival of a troubled life;better the tramp you know in the blind beggar crying out for a share of mercy whipped on the flesh of the spine to open the old scars,never to heal again,the sun will come out to play in a loving warmth on the petals of the red rose,ripe for the harvest to sleep in a bed of roses,don't cry for what society owes you,ask what you owe yourself,what do you owe a starved humanity on the brink of destruction;if you accept defeat,then you are defeated in a salute to the victorious waving the frayed flag o'er the grave of the unknown,who died for the insanity of the known lunatics,who owe you nothing in everything for themselves,statues stand tall and proud in honour of the vicious brutes gagging for the buzz in the blood of war,leaders of the planet inherit the lust in the slaughter of the starved soldier holding the gun of war to kill all human instinct in the emotion of a painful sanity,the battlefield riddled in the bullets dead in the mud to paint a window without a pane,only crippled in a defined pain,a fresco of the brave in the mud,horizontal in a shallow shadow,block out the light of life,a strange transcendence of the spirit in a blackout escape to a better place without the bullet ripping through the flesh of the peaceful soul on the run from evil,fight for the selfish people who never walked the wasted land to suffer in a crumbled wreck,a once mighty broken on the smooth rocks of the cliff face smiling in the obnoxious laugh on humanity,swing the slashing sword to dispose of the suffering wretch smashed on the rocks of a foreign land,wasted in the evil of war, you will never find peace in this place of a wasted space;drink and be merry while you can in the company of wine,women and song taken in the wild laugh of madness,a tragic reflection on humanity suffering for a worthless cause,a savage animal will eat itself into oblivion;the timeless emotion of paint on a blank canvas,a silk screen on life where once wild flowers danced in the caressing wind blowing a natural footprint on the sleeping garden of the painter's studio growing in the weeds wrapped in the cobwebs of a worn brush,stiff in the colour all dried out in the mindful eyes of the blind artist about to lose his brilliance to a delirious delirium of a forgotten memory on the blink,a triumph o'er a predicted disaster of the artist oblivious to the consequences of a lost mind,the soul soon to depart on a flight to a better place for the chosen one;hold on for as long as you can to fight the fight in the mother of all fights in the pouring rain of the darkest hour just before the dawn of a new strife, the lips glowing in a red lipstick smudged on the yellow teeth,laughing all the way to the bank of all bankers;never the twain shall meet again in never the master of your own demise,your own doom in the win of the rat race floating in a pool of your own sweat soaked in the whitest sheets on the street,now a dirty brown in the crap of a privileged life;take no prisoners on the run from the loaded gun just about to smoke a puff of anger into your gaping face for one last chance to change forever more in the cry of crocodile tears on the wrinkled cheeks,puffed in a life of pleasure fit for a squire in his own manor,answer to no one,not even yourself,the making of a good one in a good thing too good to be true,fight the fight in the last swing of the broken hand,precariously hang on the finger of the long arm smashing in a brittle crumble,fall o'er the white line as a bad loser in first place,shake the hand that shook the world,kiss the lips that smacked the world into a pouting submission,game on soon to be game over when least expected,frail in the strength of a mythical survival,smashing you into the frail arms of the darkest abyss,where the words become the beast of the night,wandering aimlessly on the blank page in the vain search of a strained inspiration,tap a riddle on the table riddled with woodworm,the skinny fingers long in a bony dance on the wood turning to dust,the human one day will be the same as the ancient trees in the dust of ashes,waiting to be blown away into the kiss of your birth;people attack you both mentally and physically in a jealous rage,furious for a violent,a fiery emotion in the head to destroy all hope of any kind of success from the now troubled mind,the ignorant will laugh into your crying face to kick you when you're down and out for the count,the dominant force of good will prevail in a powerful success,the stardust will settle in the tired mind,blast you out of the smoking barrel of an angry gun,fall on the career you never had to bounce back stronger,bigger,better than anyone else waiting to take your place,catch a break like you catch a goo goo on the run from a goo goo,no one loves you the way you love yourself;forget not the long forgotten prayer is forever humming through the mind of the firm believer on their aching knees in a quiet place,cross yourself in the name of the holy cross that's nailed to the wall of the family house, a monk afraid of himself in the past of a disturbing future,a shiver in the body is a step on the grave to shake the soul in the love of God,a year in the life of time standing in a timeless clock going tick-tock in the chime of the bell for prayer,don't cry for yourself,cry for the lost soul,rise into life with the early bird on the high perch singing sweetly in the early morning dew on the brink of success,start a new day with the chirpy birds in song for the lone stranger asleep under the sheltering branch,the olive branch of peace to all who sing with the birds,the last breath of the night in the first breath of the morning to smile on the seagull perched outside your window pane,live for the time of the moment bursting in the mind,in the written words on a blank page,painted in the love of black and white in a caring heart;the yellow meadow in full bloom will always be there for you in the four season playing out on the priceless violin,resting under the chin of a precocious talent,drink from the cup of love and hope and the light will drink for you one day when least expected, give yourself away in a bonfire to the other side,the young now worry more than the old,live every day as it comes and you'll survive the wrath of life in the lost garden coming back to life in full bloom;the star is sublime in the splash of paint dripping on the blank canvas of the mind,a niche in the strength of a six inch nail,bent in a twisted coat of silver,paint in black to stare at it long enough to turn a brilliant white, there's a price you'll have to pay in the end,at the very end of the thin line,the path once walked by the dead is now walked by the living dead in a shadow play,a real thing hidden in the truth,walk,keep walking until you can run no more,find your way out of the dark place in the clap of the hand for the echo to set you free,people walk all around you in a frightened blindness;the sexy woman dressed in the high stiletto to tease you back into the land of the living,stay away from the maze cluttered with lost people on the run from their own shadow;the trickle of water from the rusty tap is a constant leak to sedate you in a blast from the past,a soothing therapy to keep the hungry wolf from the battered door,a fierce madness bulging in the sore eyes of the dry sockets,take a slurp of boiling hot tea in the cosy tea room,flash a sweet smile to the lady with the curnie bun in the dollop of fresh cream,ready for the taking in a crispy bite of the yellow teeth,ponder awhile in the caress of the china cup on the lost moment,a fleeting chance of success laughing at you in a vacant stare;draw yourself out of the mire by the raw flesh of the missing fingernails curdled in the stale blood of the depraved,the spirit soaked to the skin for the pain to emerge when least expected,drift into moonlit night to find the perfect glow of light,subtle and fine in a refined ambivalence to take you away,far away to another place,high on the hill of the deep mountain,the crazy cat trapped in the mad dog of a bitter life,never to be sweet again in the solid silver stained in a tarnish of gold,gone under the pounding hammer for the first into the last time, look back and it's all over in the blink of a blind eye, vacant in the empty room,resting on the landing of the broken stairs leading to nowhere,fast in a furious demise to swing round and round until you fall off the merry go round on the swing touching the sky, a natural roof o'er the head in the house of the world, a welcome squat without a cause,the dim light in the head flickers in a random madness but will never burn out in the effervescent candle to proudly glow in the howling wind battered by the fierce rain;a love on the rocks of a relationship cut in the stone of a chip off the auld block of marble chiseled by the deft hand into a hunk of muscle;black on white in a colour mirage to dart through the glass eye,frame me to frame yourself in the dock of the man in the curly wig,the Good Friday of the month until the end of time,the powerful locomotive ploughs along the metal track at full speed ahead in a gush of steam to melt the flesh,a sustainability from the time of yore no more;words flash from the shadow in a bouncing tangle of a crossword on the tattered paper blowing around the crossroad of doom;the concept is burning in the light of the blinding mirage,penetrate for the first time into the missing void of a hit and miss moment flashing through the troubled mind to procreate into the elastic blast from the roar of the hungry lion in a burning desire of the bulging loin,a slap in the face full in the stress of a losing struggle with life on the run,on the go,on the brink in the blink of an eye locked in a vacant stare of delusion covered in thick layers of fat on the blubber of fate;the wheezing lungs cry out for mercy as the dry throat tightens in the rasping voice gasping for breath,hell hath no fury like a woman scorned,naked of a pride in the bed of a greedy man, shackled to the emotion of abuse,you reap what you sow,so they say with a wry smile to mess with your mind in the eclipse of a sensible understanding,a delicate reality of the body out of the skin to form a new life in a better skin,the new scales break free from the bone to blow away in the humid air;the lust, the greed in the avarice where the paint never dries on the canvas hanging on the wall of a wretched man, crying like a baby for his beloved mother,the grinding of the dirty teeth on the bleeding gums,flash a frightening smile on the naked gums;time waits for no one in the mysterious reclamation of the lost time to start over again in the old timer reading a wet page on the throne as his talent gushes away in the sewer of his choice in the making;a craved addiction in second to none,a pebble dash on the throne in the swipe of the finger to cleanse the body,it's all over apart from the shouting scream of the witch casting a spell on you,a slave to you unto me,cast the net to catch the big fish in the fishnet smooth on the long legs,silky suave in the dance of the red stiletto,a moment to cherish forever more the pale rider on a dying horse, the black ice cracked by a wicked punch crying out for mercy,the battered drum beating out a dire warning to repent,genuflect before it's too late,the scroll of love stuck to the high ceiling,staring at the girl with the blue eyes full of tears about to flow into the salt of the sea for the sinned sinner,never to wear the white veil o'er the happy face,a tangled love lost to the dark night in the howl of the hungry wolf on the hunt for the lost love of a begrudged life;

the scrotum covers the vagina in a hissing kiss from the past birth of celestial bliss,give life to the raging storm on the rampage to drown evil out of the water, to purify the soul,still in the light of the day soon to be a shadow of the night,work if you ever work at all,too lazy to rest in the bed to sleep your life away,the artificial ink on the nib to scrape words on white paper in the stroke of the paint soaked on the brush,a controlled splash from the blinkered mind,the image twisted within the image,another image to be imprisoned in the blindness of the lost image warped in the mind,a branded image in the rawness of the flesh,the reality will free the inhibitions in the click of a broken finger,clap in the vibrant echo of the rough hands;hide in the forest of the dark wood in the snap of the brittle branch,hanging low to slap too hard in the ghostly face,the pounding heart smashing through the ribs to free the aching soul,too late for the tears of mercy to save the flesh from a burning damnation; the angels protect you from the evil of the war torn mind waiting for judgment day to burn through the sky,the eyes wide shut in tears of regret to sizzle the bright flame of the glowing candle into a horrid grope of darkness,open the eyes only to go blind in a gaping retribution on humanity;establish the truth in the words of wisdom from the person towering in the belief of hope liberated in the power of love,the freedom of love for everyone with a warm heart,the person with a cold heart will muscle their way into a vacuum of love to deny the righteous a fair crack of the whip for the cat of nine tails to rip through the loving flesh denied of all emotion in the orgasmic bliss,a flushing dart through the snapping spine in a show of strength,people will laugh straight into your face for the sly stab in the back,if you tumble and fall,bounce back up in a gulping breath of survival,a fist pump to clear the head,fight another day in the life of the lone survivor;a fistral flush in the head to ride the crest of the wave,the feet tickle in the gush of the hissing bubbles about to pop on the soft flesh to be engulfed by the whiteness of the water rolling into a pounding crescendo to free the soul into the deep sea, a wet dust rising from the bed of the abyss,sleep yourself into the perfect dream,the idyllic life with the whale taking you to a better place;winter is the spring erection of summer in the softness of the autumn's death knocking on heaven's door,a natural intellect is way better than a fake tan that will eventually blotch the skin into a faded patchwork of a tainted vanity bleeding the pants of a stark denial of a botched job soon to fail,best to stick with the heavy makeup and be done with it for once and for all,a triptych,a dick in the shape of a dickhead about to explode into his own face;stretched out on a long,slender couch covered in the skin of a slaughtered beast shot in the prime of life,now extinct in the barrel of the smoking gun,cut to pieces by the knife of the trophy hunter,rolling in the greed of the bloodied money,the bulging eyes of the beast starved of life,staring intently at the obese hunter puffing on a cigar too small for the gobby mouth,stiff in a wry pout to the fallen beast of the jungle;

you are not the only one to suffer in the last of the deranged delinquents to burn at both ends of the flaming candle,fiercely throughout the barren night; blonde on blonde,brunette on brunette,redhead on a fiery redhead,clean shaven to the bone of youth,the culture flowing down the pan,fly the roost to leave the burning nest to follow the star along the furrow of the glowing sky,dig the worn heels into the bouncing cloud of nine into six,back into the nine of goodnight to greet the dawn of a new day;grasp the stinging nettle in the soft hand with a firm grip to avoid the pain of life waiting to possess you to dig the grave of youth into the old age of a crumbled life on the run from itself;climb the steep slope of the high stairs, drifting into a landing not big enough to swing a cat,a black cat on the prowl for the elusive bit of luck stuck to the blanket of the banker,drunk on the money of others down on their luck;the face of the good looking boy,scarred in the deep cut of the scumbags on the rampage,hiding behind a cowardly hoodie,never to return in the retro side of a pretty face,poles apart in the eye of the beloved mother,searching for the ambiance still in the ambiguity of a travesty slashed in the pretty face of a strange youth lost in a foreign land;me to you in you slashed in a kickback to me,a distorted image to make a loving mother cry for her beloved child destroyed for life,the only life the child can live with or without his mother,the scumbags walks away in a blissful ignorance to slash through life,go on the hunt for the lost face,sadly turned into the mud of dust,hiding on the dark side of the moon, sleep in the shadow of a defined darkness to hide in the face of humanity;love will tear you apart in a yelping cry for more of the same,again and again and again until the well runs dry to light the fire in the shrinking lion too tired to sleep in the bed made by the desert;the stigmata will cure you of the self inflicted wounds,the gaping wounds of the conflict, floating around in a lost space,like a fallen leaf in the wind of change to reap what you sow,even if the crop of the harvest has failed to deliver a single grain of wheat for the weeds to flourish in the hard times for the seed to grow into a powerful force,dodge the asteroid heading straight for you in the old school of retribution,life on the run from a stark reality gone good in a certain badness to stare the mire in the face without a view,a lost identity in the slow melt of the raw flesh,a hole in the head leaking grey matter through a snot in the nose;the warm breath fades away in the night of the morning dew drops dripping down the window pane of the innocence asleep inside the protected room of the loving mother,cooking the food of life for her only child,inside out in a painful birth to carry the cross to the other side of a better life;cold as ice sucking on the bosom so warm and nice in a farewell goodnight,lash out on the person you love the most,beaten black and blue in a mystical shade of pink,the red lips hissing through the harsh words grinding through the hoarse voice of the dry throat about to cough it all away in a spit of blood straight from the wheezing lungs about to call it a night with the girl of your dreams come true, then you snap out of it into a cold sweat of a wet dream to seal your fate,a bloody state of affairs,bad can never be any good in a crash waiting to happen to the shy child blamed for everything and anything, come,come now,it may never happen but could happen to the brightest star in the darkest sky of the frosty night;a brooding figure,a diminished figure,a straddled figure,a strange figure,a strutted figure,a warped figure in a stooped gazing pose,the emaciated figure of strife,a bewildered figure blinking in the lashes of the glass eye,two figures locked in a human guise in the leaking of juices from the hot tap,the hard figure gone soft in the head,a crouching figure in a hot release,a figure with ink on the face,a distorted face figure scarred for life on the rampage from the horrid image in the mirror,a blind faith figure,a solo figure,a sick figure,a painted figure afraid of itself going stark naked mad,a figure with the headlights on full blast to let the dog see the rabbit dying a painful death,a solo figure for life to love itself unto death do it part,a ghostly figure in the haunted house of the green gates wide shut,the quarry hole figure holding a fishing rod o'er the dark echo of storm water,a life figure devoid of life on a cold slab,a marble figure with a nail in the coffin,the blank figure with no pants,the shackled to the wall figure,the figure with sleep in the sore eyes, the horse figure without a tail,the smashed figure in the ground of no land,a helplessness figure afraid of the shadow on the flaking wall,a drunk figure on the dirty floor,a shadow figure in the dark alley at night,a figure with muscle in the soft flesh of a juicy abyss, a lady figure of the night,a figure too old to die,a figure never to lose its grip on reality,a figure to understand,a nightmare figure,a figure stroking a brush soaked in paint,a figure of impulse,a figure on the move,the austere figure,a radical figure,a warmonger figure,a deprived figure,a sinister figure,a textbook figure,a trout pout figure,a turbulent figure,a contorted figure in a wrestled grope,a dizzy figure,a deluded figure,a painted figure,a hated figure,the million pound broke figure,a severe figure,a severed figure,a stretched figure,a seated figure,the moral figure of immortality,a gallery figure,a horse of a man figure,a sexual figure,a depicted figure,a shady figure, a bald figure with hair behind the clothes,a figure in the naked room,a dead figure story,a roulette figure,a nailed figure,a painful reality figure,a wasted figure,a secret figure,a gay figure in man and woman,a six to one in half a dozen of the other,the love figure never to be loved in love,a callous figure,a tool bag figure,a pain in the hole figure,a hole in the head figure,a pedantic figure,the silent figure,a sinister figure,a survival figure,a groping figure,a natural talent figure, an expressive figure,the expensive figure,a screaming figure,the savage animal figure,a sleeping dog figure,a sewer figure,a fifty nine figure,a bird of prey figure,a beached whale figure,a nightmare figure,a sleeping figure,a guise figure,a muse figure,a hideous figure,a fairy figure,a spaced figure,a born to die figure,a raw cosmic figure,a figure of grandeur,a windy figure,a figuratively speaking figure,a retro figure of modern intent,a fascist figure,a bewildered figure, a contact figure,a wasted figure,a kick in the face figure,a naked mind figure in a car crash on the rocks, a quiet slip to the other side,the staring headlights torment the face of the slippery cliff falling into the adoring sea in the open arms of the pounding wave, gushing you into the deep abyss,the soft skin pocked in the barnacles of a hard life gone soft in the wisdom of the pouting fish to kiss the boat of the lost fisherman about to jump into the blue sea,the flagellation of the flaying arms smash into a broken demise on the rocks of doom,the off the wall of the cliff's paranoid face in the mirror of a madman on the run from his own evilness,the shimmering of the fading light on the blink of a blinkered life,the wall comes tumbling down to ride the crest of the rising wave about to crash back into the wall;the naked mind howling like the hungry wolf,shake the crying head into the open hands,a gentle caress to ease the violent pain back into a stark reality,a menace unto yourself,a flash in the black pan,never to be clean again,dead on you shivering legs soon to be dead in the sweaty bed,insomnia will keep you alive without a kick,waiting to depart on the slow train to nowhere in the first class carriage of obscurity,a selective abuse on the tortured mankind of a discarded humanity,go your own way holding a white stick,tapping it on the dark streets of a wasted place in a dreadful time for all to see,the sound of life is more vivid to the blind, without too much of a visual attack on the people with perfect vision refusing to see,to embrace life,not hate it with a vengeance,take it as it comes,change life in the face of a fabled makeshift,a makeup that will eventually wash away in the flood of the stormy water gushing through the mind of disturbia,a distortion of the flesh on the brittle bone,hanging on for as long as you possibly can endure in the irony of a self inflicted demise;the buzz of the strummed six string on the silver frets of a rock solid neck stretched to the limit of a warped hysteria in the production of a thunderous noise,the killing avalanche in the echo of the powerful feedback to the brain,the masses of the classes clash in the empty stadium to hear the choir sing in harmony to the freedom of music,if only for a fleeting moment,a glancing blow to the senses of the vile system so corrupt to the person walking the street, dressed in the rags of the greedy rich walking in the backyard of the wealthy elite,the best tainted group in society,the powerful elite go to war on the peasants of society to cramp their style,the dirt poor will never be in the realm of the filthy rich;spit the mucus into the dirt of the dust of the worn path leading to nowhere, leave the dry mouth in the speed of light,driving the demented into a senile state of no return to the land of the living,waiting for the last train to leave the hard station of life,soon to be on the blink,on the run with the hounds to hunt the fleeing hare;bounce strife off the wall of life to live forever in the bursting bubble of your belated glory,imprisoned in the depraved mind, shackled to the sleeping brain,paint the image of yourself in the menstrual blood of the biological clock going tick-tock in the dark with eyes wide shut to scream abuse at the breaking light of a new dawn;

drink and be merry while you can to stave off the consequences of inevitability ripping you apart in the painful decline of the mind and body on the rampage with each other,resilient to the law of the state,pissing all over the slate,the roof o'er the head of the alien, the backbone of the state,a society in hiding,a banana republic on the rack of extinction,the people leave in their droves,find solace in a civilized land,the tip of the iceberg melts on the dry land of a desolate place, isolated forever more,smoke the incense of life to ease the pain of poverty,take you away to a special place where the mighty fall from grace;clap the cold hands in the echo of Poets Way,with soft foot on the cobbled street to inspire the words of wisdom to sleep on the blank space,the cream will always rise to the top of the blood thicker than water,the clock that never chimes to greet the stranger sat on the slippery steps of the educated hill;the pink of the flamingos burst into a glorious flight on a delicate wing soaring high into the protective clouds,leave the salt of the water behind in a flight to freedom;the saw tooth craggy as a jagged stone to sharpen the saw back to life to fight the fight in the bare knuckles of the bleeding hands stuck to the smooth blade of the saw,now brave to cut to the bone with a sharpened saw tooth,the dust of the broken stone to settle in the raucous cough of the choking lung full in the blood of a potent stare,kiss the saw tooth back to life in the smash of the blunt hammer to shape the blade into a sharp warrior about to shoot o'er the top of the battlefield,full in the dead trees of a dying wood,the soul to drift away into the foggy mist of a soft day through a shamed window to shine on the bright side of the moon;all is fair in love and war,but only when the fat lady sings for one and all in the same tone of voice,a watch to roll with in the time of day throughout the dark night, sleep with one eye shut,stuck to the roof of the eye in the false lash,time will allow you to grow long hair on the bald head,the obese flesh to shiver on the bone, the glint in the bloodshot eye,so tired and almost blind in the confusion of work without making any money from the fabled talent on the rack in the stench of a rotten realization of an imminent doom,the defeated walk away with the wagging tail between the bandy legs,the big C branded on the wrinkled forehead,an old hag of a sweaty brow,put your inhibitions on the long tooth of the broken fingernail,the dirt hiding in the cracks of the papery skin;spin the square wheel until it stops and the silver ball dives into the air,play the mad game to be any good at all,play with paint in the splash of words in the vibrant mind,rich in the letters muddled together,like dogs linking arms on a windy day in the park,the rattle of the bark in the swirling wind,a slap on the musty cushion in the rise of a blinding dust,a choking cough to free the lungs of a starved state in the crippled mind;the magic mushroom living on the merry go round to fly high into the starry night,hit the road in a gasp of dust to crumble into the dirt of a cruel existence,turn rejection into a longing success of a wicked desperation,survive at all cost to crawl on all fours with the lame horse,struggling to make the grade in the high jump o'er the burning fence,the defeated walk away to fight another day in the sunshine of someone's garden full in the weeds of a painful neglect,rise to the occasion,ride the lame horse to the finish line of a perfect life,drink yourself sober under the wet table in a snore of perfection on the rocks,thrash your mind,not your body,back into the soul of you being human,if only for a moment or two, the macho in the man to appear in the rear mirror of a speeding car too fast to control,a shocking way to escape into the realm of madness,a gladness to ease the pain,jump from the high horse on to the slimy perch,back down to earth in a free fall through the bluest sky of the darkest day,blind as a bat to spread the virus in a blind knock on the open door;the grotesque disregard for the innate talent in the technique of chance in the trial of the error taking you to a strange place where strangers dare to venture on vulture digging into a decayed carcass,a transformation of chaos to walk in unison with the shadow hiding in the corner of a shivering life,a greed for life tangled in a trapped vulnerability laughing into your scarred face,the contaminated knife that destroyed your life in the slash of the arm possessed by the evilness that people do to each other,without any rhyme or reason,dark in the delusional mind of the delinquents on the rampage against the society that owes them nothing,but a barrage of contemptuous ignominy from the barrel of a smoking gun;a distorted mind bulging through the sore eyes bloodied in the sinister smile of a controlled dominance o'er the generosity of others too good for

for their own good,a welfare in the hands of the people waiting to manipulate in horrid abuse on the feeble righteous,slam the door shut in the innocent face of a cruel fate on the run from certain doom to fall head over heels in love with the aggressor,march away to the beat of the drum pounding a painful delirium in the head waiting to explode into the deep abyss;a mind lift that went totally wrong in the swing of the blunt scalpel on the brain inside the pumping head,weary and tired of not having a stranglehold on life in the fight of survival,there is always a piece of work behind a masterpiece about to fall off the wall in a grain of dust,the broken heart will never mend and return to the days of yore with the door never closed, ponder not on the ghostly burden of the frayed mind, haunted by the hard road rising to greet you in a bunch of fives,knock yourself in and out of a conscious decision to carry on down the road of hard knocks;the organic bliss grows within and not without someone else naked and afraid of the escaped monster on the evil rampage,most come from the bottom of a lustful desire,struggling to explode in the heat of the moment,fill the cup for a soothing drink,placate the sticky desire in a wild kiss of joy,sweetie then becomes even more sweet,stuck with the sugar of lust forever more the merrier,the animal in the human,the flash of the snarling teeth in the mad dog of war,dripping in the blood of a banished humanity;art is art for the paint never to dry in the words of a profound wisdom,soaked in the blood of failure,blue for you on you,within you,without you,Mr Blue would never have been born at all in the cold clap of the wet hand on the soft bottom of a painfully birth,the after birth lochia,green in the life of the child,asleep on the warm milk of the beloved mother,a shock to the system still bleeding in the birth of life,cry,cry,cry,cry, never stop crying the tears of a golden strife,the green will soak into the growing bones,stronger day by day in the morning dew of the breaking of day,a new day on the distant horizon,waiting to go down with the burning sun to be a new day somewhere else beyond the vast darkness;the personality of the violent snarl locked behind the gaping bars of a rusty demise until the end,show some remorse before it's too late in the day of the long nightmare,the distorted mind streams through the contorted face afraid of its imminent fate, kick your can out of the face all over the place to annoy the disturbia of the damn place,to be is to be alive in a death mask,stranger than life itself in the changing of the face through time never to stop for no man on the noisy march of life,fall in love with the bony hand that feeds you in the broken spike of bones piercing through the skin,the story will be told in the scary stare of the cracked mirror,clinging on for dear life flaked on the wall,the animal instinct stolen by the vicious greed of man hanging on the slippery slope of a disturbed extinction,screaming for a reprise in a delayed reaction,the grope of the long fingers sink into the blubber of the shivering flesh,a jelly to relish in a gulping lament,sweep the violence under the carpet of peace,show your true colours in the taste of the simmering tart coated in a fur of cream;

lick it clean,dry of all iniquity in the test of the pudding for the taking,dredge the emotions from the beginning of time,the silt will drain through the greyness,the man who left a trail of destruction in his wake,never to take the blame,thousand of years in the making,life flashes before the blind eyes,the dry flesh drips on the raw canvas,a black whiteness drags a haunting brush o'er the wetness of the exposed canvas,spread the long arms to the bony hands in a tender massage to paint the glorious words on a finished canvas,a stillness of the avant garde lost in the reflection of the glass, the slime of a mulled despair stained in a yellow mist,abusing some for the gain of others in a selfish game;touch the red lips in a fleeting glance,a stretched kiss never to reach out to the pouting lips gagging for some more,embarrassed by the laughing mirror,the rotten teeth ready to pop out of the shriveled roots of old age,the gummy smile stuck to the mirror for the last time,the lost moment carved in the opaque transparency,hard as a rock to smash the glass jar,a voluptuous trap in the making,remove all the clothes to reveal a naked surprise,a scarecrow in the making,stand tall in a big field of honey rip for the picking,the eye for an ear for a tooth full in the decay of the face,the stretched canvas of a ripping skin in every thread to stitch the deep scars in the swipe of the brush saturated in the paint to plaster o'er the cracks of the loose skin never to be taught again in the image of youth,a young lad grasping the stinging nettle in full flight out of the auld place to seek the freedom of the refined world waiting in the welcome of open arms for the tortured soul, rich in the shyness of a fresh beginning to kick all of the troubles away in the wind of change,blowing o'er the streets paved in gold,the myth of the old girl sat by the hearth of the open fire,blazing in a fierce glory for the young lad to come good after leaving the warmth of the mountain fire;ride the black stallion to a glorious victory o'er the faded line,once so white to blind the eyes into a saving squint,the sweat of the wrinkled brow rubs dust into the weeping eye,bleed in the bloodshot of the ugly image life has to offer the good living soul on the run from the chasing ruination in a mocking scream;the ivory rolls into a pitched beat on the grand piano of the pauper to be buried in the ebony of the mausoleum,a vault fit for the righteous, the skinny combover of the writer with its head on the block,the money flows into the swishing crack of the whip on the posterior of life,the toughest skin turning red in a raging fury,the incessant cry of the whip ripping the flesh away in the dawn of a new birth;the hissing snake is coming to get you,dead or alive,it will gobble you away in the suction of hunger,the masked slap of the unauthorized kick in the soft flesh of the stinking pants;work less to fritter the life away in a fast car running out of petrol,just before an accident waiting to happen,a mean dreary floats o'er the anti climax of the situation in a stationary crash,the charcoal of the shorthand stained in the fingers of the longhand scraping the black nails on the page with blurred words written between the lines in the back of the mind,scrub the page like a tired scrubber on a fast walk down the hard road,hoping to make a bob or two or even bump into Bob looking for a damn good time while he can last in the passing of time,the flick of a coin,coated in the dirt of crime;the life of an artist trapped in the work of another artist,steal what you can,while you can in the puff of the rosy cheek,if you allow the swinging arm of the artist to slap you in the sodden face,then immediately vacate to crack the whip of your own fate,get into your own mindset when you vacate the boredom of yore,only to be on the run from an everlasting confrontation with the crack in the tainted mirror,a sabotage in the making to seal your fate;wear the boot a size too big to skin the sole of the soul,the wasted skin to feed the desire of an organized progression to gain a positive beat of the heart,working flat out for the master of its life,the moustache handles stab you in the eye,crazy people create a confused burden on people trying to help them to live a normal life,a hearse for a short journey, a hearse for a horse drawn carriage in the final journey through life,a penny to keep the eyes closed,ready for the final ride home,a day in the life of anyone alive and kicking into the stride of survival, taking it to the other side;try to arrive before you leave,say a farewell in a firm handshake,walk away in the appropriate moment,vanish into the ghostly mist of the inviting night,hissing in the flicker of the haunting tongue,blind to the danger of the fangs lunging into the naked flesh,the poisonous juice flowing in the froth of the withering mouth,the red lips of curdled blood smile in a momentary laugh on the yellow teeth smudged with the lipstick of the stuck lips still bleeding in the scarred smile of a long run for your life without a stumble into the waiting pain,the aroused flesh throbs through the brow,dripping in a blinding sweat to drown the eyes in the crying tears of sorrow;throw a penny of spare change into the echo of the bucket,begging for a strangled mercy to take the pain away,before the demons arrive on the scene of the crime,scream it out in a gush of saliva to hit the floor covered in a carpet of sawdust,stumble around the dark room with the long arms outstretched to touch the flaking wall of the house with the door banging in the eerie draft leaking through the hall of mirrors,the rusty hinge falls to the floor to sleep in the darkness forever more,the white stick hitting the ghost going stone mad in the dust of the flaking wall;the morphine kills the pain in the head so much that you end up dead in a heap without knowingly aware it ever happened,it was only meant to be a quick nap in the sweaty bed,then to walk away into another room of your strange life,without the intention of the big sleep,a leafy shiver should boost your dreary existence back into the land of the living, only for it to be a natural occurrence again and again and again on the run from the paranoia in the warped head about to drop off the scale of discovery;take you back to the cradle,rocking you into a controlled equilibrium with the old women making funny faces in a laughing snarling madness,leaving the victim stifled in a traumatized delirium;the flapping wings of the hungry bird hovers o'er the flaking wall to dig the sharp talons into the whiteness of the bombastic ghost squealing for mercy,the powerful wings gushing in a spreadeagle pose to float the ghost away to the land of fire and brimstone,the hinge doesn't creak anymore in the closing of the door in silence,a fabled slap on the hand in the face of humanity,hanging on the imaginary rope dangling from the bluest sky,the will to survive is vibrant in a surge through the veins, the dust of the flaking wall has reached the dizzy heights of the clouds,a slow crumble of the wall to fade away into the tall grass of the sky;the sensation of the pleasant peasant suddenly turns into the evil, nasty beast shouting abuse at everyone sinking in the same boat,foolish enough to listen to the sprayed words of violence,the wicked mind dressed in a naked rife of delusion on the society of its birth,the hairy bush wet in the corner of the wild garden growing stronger in the weeds of nature,the weeds that slowly strangle you into a gagging hatred for nature as it appears from the dirt of the soil,clip the bush back to life in the early buds of a saturated spring in love with the winter of a late summer,gushing a warmth on the colour of a stifled autumn throwing a refined caution to the long sleep in the sweaty bed;the sad tale of the mad dog running around in circles to find the missing tail that used to wag him back to life,the story of the missing tale goes on and on and on,never to cease,to stop when the light turns red in the anger of life,hold the cold hand on the warmth of the heartbeat,a palpation to caress the patient into a cold sweat,a strong palpitation in the fluttering heart, the pumping of blood through the clogged veins, drifting through the suffering body in a twitching ache to take you by the bony hand of strife,it's good to be alive to greet the breaking of a new day,blind in the drip of the dew from the green leaf of spring on the mend to walk around the bend of the hard road that will never rise to meet you,ease your way into the next room,force yourself to relax to dream the dream where the head is soft on the pillow to dream the impossible dream,wash away the sweat in the faded sheet of the sodden bed,musty in the life of the mind in a constant exile on a deserted land,a landscape ravaged by the limping earth,the stagnated gaze of the blind eye before the savage penetrating of the mind in the flesh,the nature of the unnatural mind is to abuse the same victim,innately,over and over again and again in the life of an evil brute on the loose in a warped reality,the state falls asleep in the snore of the beast thrashing the innocent mind into a designed submission;take you back to the egg to start all over again in a completely different surround,alien to the person of yore with the ink stained hand,the left hand frowned on in the eyes of the educated fool,keep moving around the circle to become the full circle in the upside down image to fall head over heels in love with the image in the mirror,sleep awhile in the dark room to dream your life away in the blind blink of the opaque eye,the cataract in full bloom on the focus of the stare,a piercing gaze into the unknown matter flying around the space of the mind,a virile lewdness gone soft in the head in the overdose of life to sleep it off and away,the image of the meat will dwell in the mind of a certain demise,a decay of all that ever mattered in the greyness of the dark room,the matter goes blank in a raw blandness on the blink in the squint of the sore eye,the groping of a bulging fact,an infatuation of a person that will never reciprocate in the gesture of a favourable kiss on the red lips of a glossed existence;the volcanic sand turns into a black dust,the rear of the skull smashed on the edge of the formica table,dry in the blood of wet bone leaking in the tears of the unfortunate moment,lucky to be still alive all those years later in a distant land where the streets are professed to be paved in gold,a fools gold to make you feel rich in the greed of the filthy rich on the march for even more wealth,the leaving of a land on the run from a fierce destruction,a wildfire lit by the shameless corruption of a blinkered state that will burn itself into a charcoal of dust in the pure dirt of the soil pumping in the heart of the people,the land will survive the nuclear blast in the political air,a drama dressed on the floor of a creaking stage,sleep in the corner of the empty room,a tearful reminisce of the auld country on the brink of disaster in the eyes of many,ignored by the few holding the magic wand,whip the skin off the broken spine of a land so beautiful to tear it apart,the land still young in the old age of a troubled mountain to climb in the bare feet of a poor soul,stooped in the youth of regret on the rusty rack smashed on the creaking floor of the stage,love the land that never did you a bit of harm,a land that offered a gentle slap at the birth of the crying baby, soon to cry in the youth of old age,within and without the mountain by your side in times of strife;born again in the life of the concrete jungle,where people look at you with disdain,a sanity on the brink of madness to fade in and out of a refined conscience,stay away until you die,return with a grey beard,the tail blowing in the wind,wash the goodness out of the beard in the splash of cold water,the hairy face wet as a sewer rat in the making,a powerful swimmer in the stank waters gushing from the human body;bleak in the stain on the finger tips of lost lovers still locked together in a blissitude of exquisite seminal bites on the rough tongue,flickering on each other to linger in the mind forever more the virgin of the wave gurgling in the salt of the juices,potent in the sea of life,surfing on the cusp of the dancing wave,rolling into a world of fabled dreams to be awoken on the slippery rocks of a crushed doom,alone now in a down and out pool to swim with the dead fish,once the life of the sea,the smooth bone,bare to the raw flesh,the skin eaten by the stinging crabs crawling into the bleeding flesh for the kill;the end of the road for the forbidden lovers on the last legs of the sinned sinners,a tragic comedy in the making of your dreary life for most austere folk,sat in a boat floating aimlessly on still water without a paddle in the hand,make babies while the sun shines on the biological clock going tick-tock in the dreary bedroom,the exotic arousal on the silk sheet for the maker to make a mark for themselves, with or without prior approval from the appropriate party,still dressed in the veil of two virgins;

let sleeping dogs lie on a bed of straw,fresh from the harvest field of the Hornet's nest,a lone buzz in the clouds,the wings covered in a stubble of dust, the memory of the long journey through life on the back of the lonely road,sat in a rocking chair with a strong gaze o'er the half door,the warmth of the air strokes the wrinkled skin on the wilted chin,a fond kiss from a love long departed,a fat bag on the shoulder to ride the pony and trap away from the place of birth,a good place,but never outstay your welcome for the vale of the mountain will suck you in and blow you away,so it's best to go your own way without a kick on the pony and trap to run away;narrow the slits of the eye to see the lines closing in on you,the crush of the words rise to greet you in the tired yawn of life,clear the stuffed head in a raucous sneeze of the flying snot to land on the cracked mirror,the walking stick worn to the brittle bone will lead you to the promised land where the righteous stay in a glorious cavern,abide by the strict rules to progress in the vigour of a stark reality staring you straight in the wrinkled face, a strange laugh from the one hiding behind the mask about to smash through the wrinkles of a stranger's life on the edge of the froth riding the crest of the breaking wave,the wild stallion of the sea,the light painted on the pounding wave faintly lit,cast a shadow on the cliff face wet in the froth of the vanished wave, a rumbling clap to still echo o'er the face of the cliff; the limitations are there for all to see,to refuse,to ridicule,to deny in a lasting embrace to mankind,a wry failure to bounce back into a sly failure next time, feel more for others than for yourself about to fall off the blank page,without even a blob of black ink to pierce through the eyes of the mind,better the devil you know than the devil you don't know at all,taste will take you to the place to ease you into a sound sleep,rise in the darkness of the morning to rest in the glow of the moonlit night shining on the sleeping face, wake to the music of the singing birds in the morning leaking through the window pane,the birds stand to attention to do their thing on the wing,put the human beast to shame;better yourself to better others in the corner of the eye,write without the scrape of the broken nib leaking in a river of ink,if you stare at the blank page long enough for something to happen then something is bound to happen in the occurrence of the perfect moment,the concept in the dormant mind soon to be aroused will take you there in the end,trust in me to trust in yourself,or forever be an outcast in the forbidden place,the capacity to think in your sleep, write the blank words in the vacant mind full of talent, bursting to escape the boredom of normality in the life of a passing day into night,the secret is never giving up on the dream,square up to the square laughing at your refined swagger,a gait to die for in the swivel of the rocking hips on the move in the human rocking chair,the grim reaper of the mind will rise in a furious roar of anguish,spit rage through the veins of the man in a struggle,a tug of war in a barren place with himself;the staggering bear with tears in the eyes of the hungry stare on the hunt for the secret lost in the dust,scattered on the hard road, the poor are nailed to the middle of the hard road without a turn in sight,a never ending journey to nowhere in the cry of the wilderness,the white light darts through the sky,a lightning waiting to flash back into the sleeping soul,the grey matter ejaculates from the stagnant mind,trapped in the shackles of a fierce addiction amassed in the bead of sweat dripping from the furrowed brow,a coldness cripples through the body,a staggered release on the moist lips failing to caress the parched tongue to smack in a kiss of hope to the future of the past that is rarely forgotten in the wretched hand shaking like a crumbled leaf,once dry and crispy in the prime of life,the young growing old fast in the precocious demise of the mind tuned like a wild beast in full flight o'er the arid desert of the wasted plains where a lushness used to roam freely; the half empty glass stuck firmly in the shiver of a strong handshake,a drink to ease the pain for a moment without any real gain in the stooped body trapped in the corner of isolation;the hungry rats flash in the sore eyes burning in a strange fire,a ring of smoke hovers o'er the open hearth fire,where the black shawl of the departed woman hangs proudly from a ceiling hook,black as soot in the choking smoke of the forefathers long gone to the grave resting on the side of the mountain;a few survive now to carry the tattered flag on the long march o'er the mountain, steeped in the history of a bloodied freedom,lose yourself deep in the wooden chair made by the man blessed with the great hands to ever touch wood,relax in the sweet smoke of the pipe to sleep the night away in a blaze of flames,a broth of porter in the hand stained in the blackness of the pipe,a hard life buried deep in the crevasse of the ancient stone,growing in the moss of the ghostly forest,a danger to the folk wandering through the forest in the darkest hour before the dawn,for the evil mist of the hour may take you away with the fairies;a fiery fury spits in a hissing retribution,a protection to the folk asleep inside the wood cottage of the ancient mountain,loose the last drop of blood if you stray into the darkest hour before the dawn of a new day in the mad dance of the jiving flames gushing through the broad chimney,the cinders still glowing in the heat of the savage battle in the imaginary battlefield,rekindle the smoking embers of the dying fire with a stabbing stoke of the hay fork,a two pronged bite into the flesh of the precious fire, the forefathers gone to a better place,leave the great land abused by the state,never to return until the day of judgment to separate the wheat from the chaff in the fierce gnashing of teeth,naked in birth to be naked in death,a certain demise to the eventual bang on your door, holding the number of your imminent fate when you take the last gasp of breath,dust you shall return;the man you know is better than the woman you don't,the woman you know is better than the man you don't,the person you gave life to in a moment of madness will return the favour one day in a ghetto,shackled to a towering slum of the weakest link trained to grow muscles that blow the mind into a screaming wisdom,awoken by the rumble of the thunder waiting to strike a furious clap for humanity, the earth burning alive in the flesh of the people,the virus is coming to get you,variant after variant,after variant,your luck will soon evaporate into the polluted air of the flaming ozone layer,the shield now banished into outer space to play with the universe;burn alive in the molten fire of the sun,within,without the metal bars bent in the heat of your prison,the moment of freedom has gone up in smoke,run away to be someone,to be somebody's child still on the run from the growing shadow,a monkey on the back of the crippled spine,laugh at your own madness,scribble indelible words on a blank page to blow away in a windy draught under the half door,nailed to the busted frame in a six inch nail of rust to whistle through the wind of a bitter change;the leaf still crispy on the branch about to snap in the finger of the old man puffing on his pipe in a sweet smoke to life and the living dead once alive and still alive in the cherished memory;pick up the pace of life in the gurgling lungs of the planet on the move,on the run from a fatal explosion to blow the mind away in the powers that be hidden in the vaults of the dark web,if you ever become high as a steeple,the only way out is down in a treacherous fall from grace to crash into the roar of the vicious bear;it was never like that in my day,the day when life stood still in the slug on the cup of milky tea,hand in hand with the beloved mother still in love with the empty cradle,longing for the good old days to make a noisy return,the best has yet to come in the belated rumble of the loin,allow the stank mind to breathe in the natural flow of puberty, without the stifling smell,take a lunging breath to fill the lungs with hope,a rich vitality in the destination unknown with a tattered ticket to ride in the wet hand of stale sweat,hide in the shadow of the iron clad station,wait for the opportune moment to ride the steam train of the merry go round,taking you to a weird place so strange for even a blind stranger;a red fox,old in the emaciated grey coat,jumps the fence in a limping leap o'er the graffiti held together by paint,a flicker of the long tongue licks through a puddle of slimy water,green in the many conflicting shades of a rich colour,the wag of the bushy tail sails the fox away to a safe place,animal life tame in the concrete jungle, walk pass you on the way home to greet his partner in crime asleep in the dim den,wear the mask of the fox to survive on the wing of the gliding peregrine falcon,digging the sharp talons into the prey of life,the heavy drinking fox stops for a quick slug on the green water,still slimy in the pool of the stagnant pond,a kiss of life on the small lips,regurgitate the sewer rat to feed the other half,still asleep in the den,dim in the blink of the bloodshot eyes,the survival of the fittest in the jungle,missus fox only goes out in the dead of the moonlit night,the red lipstick on the alluring lips to match the heavy make up on the hairy face,a feline swagger down the road leading to the park,lush in the dance of the young pretender on the hunt for the teasing missus fox,a slap in the snarling face with the bushy tail to put the young lad in his place,no hanky panky tonight for the flirting missus fox,her fella waiting in the dim den for a kiss of the red lips, home is where the heart grows fonder in the miss of a beat for the love of missus fox on the return to the den of her life,the steamy window of the night air grows stronger in the mist of the morning dew;quarrel with yourself to placate the troubled mind back to life, the mind still perforated in a polyp refusing to pop;a sunny drink in the beer garden with people taking advantage of your generosity,only to vanish in the haze when its the round of duty at the bar,a sloppy kiss in a farewell blitz,blink and you miss it forever more in search for the secret,the beer garden is long gone in the decline of the spontaneity of the missing people,bang the head back to a sane normality,bang, bang,bang and keep on banging until you reach your destination at the isolated station without a platform to perform your dance that will never leave your aching feet,going tap,tap,tap on the imaginary platform of the wild field,overgrown in weeds,never let it be said that you couldn't perform on the wild stage of the field;the thrill of the unknown destination,only to land in a shithole of shite that hits the fan,the slap of the fat hand on the baby about to cry in the gasp of the first breath,the skin soft in the blubber of flesh, hiding in the tears of life,old age is the kick start in the arse,return if you can to the blissful age of the perfect innocence,when you were afraid of the dark, sleep with the shimmering light of the fluttering flame of the white candle,run with the hare to hunt with the hounds, free diving into the deep,the long arms spiked into a V,a stroke of genius can hit you when least expected,a fart can be a leak in the pants, a right can easily be a wrong to put back right,say what you want to say and what you don't want to say, don't say it at all,a slap in the arse of the new born,soon becomes a slap in the face of the man on the run from himself,a slap in the face of a dire humanity,what you believe in then,you hate now with a vengeance,the love of your life then,will slowly vanish away in the passing of time,a smack on the lips becomes a kiss on the red lips,soon to be a tangle of tongues soak in the saliva of complete strangers,it will never happen to some who never want it to happen at all,cry out for a kiss in the leak of the stale saliva,edit a kiss into the perfect kiss on the lips saturated in the red lipstick of a controlled mind on the blink with the stark reality,understand to be understood on a stand to replace the big stage of a doomed reality;run naked to play in the shadow of the night to stagger into the dawn of another inviting day,a collage to confuse the mind,day after day,after day until the end of time,the abstract madness in the crude expressionism of a delusion splashed in the delirium of the paint,go the way of the hard road without a turn in the never ending march to a warped freedom,it will come to you when it's all too late with one foot in the shallow grave,the dust in the dirt will take you to the other side of a blank page,a blank canvas to brush your future;big is better than best in the eyes of the woman possessed by the crap of a fabled illusion of grandeur,a smirk,a smile,a wry laugh turns into an itch that cannot be scratched,a suffocation in the rasping gasp of a vaporized breath;

make the outside just like the inside of the mind in the tap of the stick on the bald head,the holy well will never run dry until the end of time,better to be still in the land of the living than to be a dead hero,unknown to the masses lost in the most famous mile,love it, hate it,people fail in the false smile,a shroud in the slaughter of the innocence;whatever you endeavour, give it the utmost attention it deserves,allow the curdled blood to flow o'er the detail to shine a light on the dormant talent,hidden away in a dark vault,a slow swell in the wave rolling into a monstrous breaker to crash on the sand of the golden beach,soak it all in to drink from the pure cup of life in the salt of the sea, born from the breaking water to die in the water of a precious gravity,he that giveth will also taketh away in the flash of the pious hand;the lover of art stroked on the sacred roof of the earth in the flesh of mankind streaked on the ceiling of humanity,keep on searching and you shall find the elusive secret of life in the gasp of the last breath,depart through the vast dunes of the desert in the weak heartbeat to take you away on the wing of a prayer,the seagull swoops low in a mighty soar to the opening sky;absurd in the absurdism to accept life as it it,take the bad by the scruff of the hairy neck when all the good has vanished into the haze of a streaking maze,red and blue with a hue of pink for you in the flutter of a heartbeat to be black and blue all over again,the distant echo of the beating drum rifles through the mind bleeding through the long nose,the broken bone twisted forever more,never again to stare at the laughing mirror;

the park bench may become your soft bed to sleep the night away beneath the twinkle of the stars,cold as ice in your hour of need,shivering in the pouring rain,the confused mind struggling to find a path to freedom,the coldness of the frost will soon warm the bones,brittle in learning how to walk again in old age,wondering where it all went wrong in the prime of life,just about able to rub the scrawny hands back to life;the sore eyes almost blind,blink o'er the watchtower,wide as an open gate leading to a vast enlightenment,the warmth in the songs of the summer birds cut short by the deep snow of a treacherous winter,the wild animals survive better than the wild humans,savage in the quest for glory in the greed of power,the yellow finger tips stained in the long nails cutting deep into the troubled soul,the dirt hiding under the ugly nails,dig deep into the itchy scalp,flaking in the dead skin of the bald head,full in the greyness of old age,the charcoal ashes of the dusty tobacco in the clay pipe,still warm on the fingers stuffing new life into the pipe,the wheezing lungs gasping in the puff of the sweet smoke from the clay pipe cracked,gone in the head,slightly mad,not the full shilling,soft in the head,brain dead for a want in the head of the poor lad,the mad stare of the wasted gaze,blind in the glass eye that cannot see beyond the broken nose,remember the childish innocence of the young lad growing old before his time,too fast for his own good,the shy boy with the golden lisp,laughing at the crying lad with the horrible stammer,savaged in a bitter lament to leave a bad taste in a mouth full of rotten teeth;

quick to judge,slow to forgive when the ball is in the other court,far away from the agricultural swing of the lunatic on the loose,rags to riches back to rags,more rags of life to land in the rag heap,a flicker of paint on the canvas to land in the eye,squinting the paint away to see more clearly now that the paint has gone back on the canvas,once so brilliant white,now covered in a thick coat of black,the pubes have vanished from the mind,only to be troubled by something else,the naked eye struggles to understand the naked body,stretched to the limit,frightened of the stalking stare in a frosty gaze of the bloodshot eye,back to the rags to fall apart on the rags,longing to burn,to go up in smoke, sleep on a bed of rags to cuddle the aching bones back to life;the wilted flower in love with you to love you always,the daisy petals to blow away,lower the thick head in shame,fall apart to pull yourself together in the final roll of the dice,the scarlet tears drip from the red eyes full of pain and sorrow ploughed into the wrinkled face,time will tell if it can be a healer,time will never stop to pick up the pieces,the legs are crippled from kicking far and wide,a penny for a roll in the hay,soaked in the seed of love,a puppy love so fabled in the shack of a lost love,full in the strife of a wasted youth,a twist in the swing of the tail,the old rope slips through the feeble hands,the crazy mind will shine on in the long journey of life,the lighthouse will guide you through stormy water,full in the salt of life, the headstone drooped on a pious slope,stand tall in a sinking land of the slanting shadow in the rising sun, ready to sleep in the dead of the night, cut down in your prime,longing for a return,but be careful what you wish for in the tired eyes of the sleeping child,kissed by the loving lips of the beloved mother,safe in the bosom of the whitest cloud of the bluest sky,full steam ahead to greet your maker;bang on the wall of the door to open the gate,taking you by the hand,all over the land,the promised land,where you can survive without the emotional pain of a physical fallout,until death do you part,the smashed mirror of yore will now bring you the best of luck;no time to delay before the hanging of humanity

www.ingramcontent.com/pod-product-compliance
Lightning Source LLC
Chambersburg PA
CBHW052116150726
48002CB00006B/2377